PRAISE FOR JESSICA DAY GEORGE

The Rose Legacy

"A fresh, original story that will warm hearts and entertain readers of all ages." —Jennifer A. Nielsen, *New York Times* bestselling author of The Ascendance Trilogy

"Set in a fascinating and fantastic new world, *The Rose Legacy* will make you long for a horse of your own!" —Sarah Beth Durst, award-winning author of *The Girl Who Could Not Dream*

"Will delight readers who love a classic-feeling fantasy, as well as those who absolutely love horses . . . This thought-provoking fantasy with relatable characters is clever and heartfelt." —*Booklist*

"A rich story with plenty of surprising plot twists and a strong undercurrent of female empowerment." —*Kirkus Reviews*

"This tale will speak to readers who feel like an outsider, as well as those who adore animals . . . Readers who love Shannon Hale's fiction . . . will be captivated by this luminous start to a new series." —*School Library Journal*

"Horse-crazy fantasy fans will devour this title and be eager for more." —*BCCB*

TUESDAYS AT THE CASTLE SERIES

"These kids are clever, as is George's lively adventure. May pique castle envy." —*Kirkus Reviews* on *Tuesdays at the Castle*

"This story puts an unexpected spin on the typical princess tale. Readers will root equally for crafty Celie and for her castle." —*Library Media Connection* on *Tuesdays at the Castle*

"There is a warmth here that is utterly irresistible." —*BCCB* on *Tuesdays at the Castle*

"A charming, adventurous story with a spirit that will appeal to fans of Kate DiCamillo's *The Tale of Despereaux*." —*Shelf Awareness* on *Tuesdays at the Castle*

"There is plenty to charm readers in this second book in the series." —*School Library Journal* on *New York Times* bestselling *Wednesdays in the Tower*

"A sweet, funny, sincere story in which siblings work together." —*Kirkus Reviews* on *New York Times* bestselling *Wednesdays in the Tower*

"Full of excitement, adventure, humor, and mystery." —*Random Musings of a Bibliophile* on *New York Times* bestselling *Wednesdays in the Tower*

"Lovely and engaging, this fantasy series continues to have wide appeal." —*Booklist* on *Thursdays with the Crown*

"Fans of the series will eagerly devour this latest installment." —*School Library Journal* on *Thursdays with the Crown*

Go, my love! Go!

Florian went. He practically flew. Even though he was exhausted, he raced along the road, parting the mists like a saint parting the waters of a sea. Anthea wove her gloved fingers into his mane to make sure she was holding tight as she reached yet again for Brutus.

They had to deliver their message, but the mist had slowed them down since they had left their last posting. They were hours behind now.

"I. Can. Almost. Find. Him." She panted into her scarf, spitting out wool. "I can—"

Florian reared and Anthea screamed. A man had appeared in the mist directly in front of them, holding something large and dark in front of his body. Anthea yanked the reins up and back and Florian nearly sat on his haunches to avoid stepping on the man. With one hand Anthea fumbled out her pistol, cursing the safety strap on the holster.

—From *The Queen's Secret*

JESSICA DAY GEORGE is the *New York Times* bestselling author of the Rose Legacy series, Tuesdays at the Castle series, the Dragon Slippers series, and the Twelve Dancing Princesses series, as well as *Silver in the Blood* and *Sun and Moon, Ice and Snow*. Originally from Idaho, she studied at Brigham Young University and worked as a librarian and bookseller before turning to writing full-time. She now lives in Salt Lake City, Utah, with her husband and their three children. Visit Jessica online at www.jessicadaygeorge.com and @JessDayGeorge.

BLOOMSBURY PUBLISHING
TITLE: The Queen's Secret
SERIES: Rose Legacy
AUTHOR: Jessica Day George
ISBN: 978-1-5476-0089-2
FORMAT: hardcover middle grade novel
TRIM: 5 1/2" x 8 1/4"
PRICE: $16.99 U. S./ $22.99 Can.
PUB DATE: May 14, 2019
PAGE COUNT: 256
AGES: 8–12
GRADES: 3–6

CONTACT: Lizzy Mason
(212) 419-5340
elizabeth.mason@bloomsbury.com

BLOOMSBURY

THE QUEEN'S SECRET

A ROSE LEGACY NOVEL

THE QUEEN'S SECRET

A ROSE LEGACY NOVEL

Jessica Day George

BLOOMSBURY
CHILDREN'S BOOKS
NEW YORK LONDON OXFORD NEW DELHI SYDNEY

BLOOMSBURY CHILDREN'S BOOKS
Bloomsbury Publishing Inc., part of Bloomsbury Publishing Plc
1385 Broadway, New York, NY 10018

BLOOMSBURY, BLOOMSBURY CHILDREN'S BOOKS, and the Diana logo
are trademarks of Bloomsbury Publishing Plc

First published in the United States of America in May 2019
by Bloomsbury Children's Books

Bloomsbury books may be purchased for business or promotional use. For information on
bulk purchases please contact Macmillan Corporate and Premium Sales Department at
specialmarkets@macmillan.com

Library of Congress Cataloging-in-Publication Data
available upon request
ISBN 978-1-5476-0089-2 (hardcover) • ISBN 978-1-5476-0090-8 (e-book)

Book design by John Candell
Typeset by Westchester Publishing Services
Printed and bound in the U.S.A. by Berryville Graphics Inc., Berryville, Virginia
2 4 6 8 10 9 7 5 3 1

All papers used by Bloomsbury Publishing Plc are natural, recyclable products made from wood
grown in well-managed forests. The manufacturing processes conform to the environmental
regulations of the country of origin.

To find out more about our authors and books visit www.bloomsbury.com
and sign up for our newsletters.

For my daughter,
A middle book for a middle child!
Just remember:
You're never too old to shout, "Horsies!"

1

THE FOREST OF ARN

ANTHEA LEANED LOW OVER Florian's neck as his hooves pounded the road. The low mist that crept out of the trees on either side of the road swirled out of their way as they passed, and closed again behind them, obscuring the way they had come as much as the way ahead. Anthea didn't like it. There was something unnatural about the mist.

She pressed her face against Florian's damp neck. He smelled like sweat and dust, and his mane whipped at her eyes. She closed them and listened to the beat of his hooves and the pounding of the blood in her ears.

Keep going, she told him. *Keep on, my brave one!*

Hold tight, Beloved.

She tugged her scarf up over her nose and mouth as protection against the mist as Florian surged forward again. Her hair fluttered out behind her—she had long ago lost the ribbon holding it back, but as long as they kept moving it hardly mattered. She shifted position again: she had been in the saddle for hours, and needed a break, but there was no time. She sat up a little and looked over her shoulder, but all she could see was mist. Florian slowed, but she urged him on.

After a few more minutes, though, they had to slow down. Anthea didn't want Florian to injure himself going flat out for too long. Besides which, the mist was thickening and she didn't want him putting a foot wrong.

I can keep running, Beloved, Florian said.

When the mist clears, Anthea reassured him. *For now, call ahead to Brutus. If you can.*

I can feel him, but I do not know if he hears me, Florian told her.

We will go closer, we will reach him, Anthea said.

Anthea cast her own thoughts ahead with the Way. She could dimly sense that there was a horse somewhere ahead, but that was all. They had never been able to re-create their feat of last year, when Florian and Anthea had reached all the way across the length of Coronam and told Constantine and Finn that Anthea was in trouble. Uncle Andrew was sure that they would be able to do it again, but so far they had not had any luck.

She lost the feeling for Brutus, but then it came back stronger. The mist was being stirred by the wind, and this section of road was as smooth as they could hope it to be, so she gave Florian a little nudge with her heels.

Go, my love! Go!

Florian went. He practically flew. Even though he was exhausted, he raced along the road, parting the mists like a saint parting the waters of a sea. Anthea wove her gloved fingers into his mane to make sure she was holding tight as she reached yet again for Brutus.

They had to deliver their message, but the mist had slowed them down since they had left their last posting. They were hours behind now.

"I. Can. Almost. Find. Him." She panted into her scarf, spitting out wool. "I can—"

Florian reared and Anthea screamed. A man had appeared in the mist directly in front of them, holding something large and dark in front of his body. Anthea yanked the reins up and back and Florian nearly sat on his haunches to avoid stepping on the man. With one hand Anthea fumbled out her pistol, cursing the safety strap on the holster.

"Who are you? What do you want?" Anthea shouted.

"Don't kill me!" the man screamed. "Please! I have a family!"

Anthea brought Florian down on all fours and backed him away from the man. She had her pistol out finally, and trained it on the dark thing the man held. He was muffled from head to foot against the mist and cold, and she could barely make out his eyes, which were wide with fear. What was that thing he was holding? And what was he doing on this lonely stretch of road, on foot, in this weather?

"Don't move!" Anthea ordered him.

"Don't let your beast kill me," the man pleaded.

"Then tell me who you are!"

"I'm an emissary for the Crown!"

Anthea took that in for a moment.

"Oh," she said, lowering her pistol. "So am I."

He slowly took in the long gray army overcoat she wore, the pistol, and the wild tangles of her brown hair. His eyes went to her face, stopped on the scar through her eyebrow, flicked down as though embarrassed, caught on the rose pin on her lapel, and grew even wider.

"They didn't say there would be a *girl*," he muttered.

"Who didn't say that?" Anthea asked, her voice sharp. "Who sent you?"

"The . . . the Crown," the man said.

Florian snorted, and Anthea felt her mouth twitch in response. "Could you be a bit more specific?" she asked. His eyes were on her pistol now, but she didn't lower it.

"The Crown," he said stubbornly.

"Where are you going?" Anthea said. "What did the Crown send you to do? Alone. In the middle of nowhere. On foot."

She looked at her watch. She could almost feel Brutus still, and it was making her testy. If this man made her even later for her rendezvous . . .

"I'm looking for the . . . the horses," the man said.

His eyes went to Florian, then slid back to her pistol. Anthea realized that this was not because he thought the pistol was more dangerous, but because he could hardly bring himself to look at the stallion. Nor did he look back at her face again. Anthea knew that her scar, while it visibly bisected her left eyebrow, wasn't hideous or disfiguring, so she guessed that what made him uncomfortable was seeing a girl riding a monster.

A girl wearing the Queen's Rose.

"Well, you've found one," Anthea said. "Now what?"

"I have to . . . to take your photograph," the man said.

"What on earth?" Anthea marveled. "Here? Now?"

"My motorcar broke down," the man explained. "I was told there was a camp of your . . . brigade . . . near here . . . ?"

"Perhaps there is," she said warily. "What is your name?"

"Er, Watson. Arthur Watson."

Anthea's attention was snagged. Was that Brutus? She reached out to him, remarking idly to the man, "I have a pet owl named Arthur."

Beloved?

What is it, my dear? Her attention snapped to Florian.

There are horses coming!

Who?

I cannot tell yet!

Where are they coming from? Is Brutus coming toward us with Caillin MacRennie?

No, they are behind us!

Once he said it, Anthea could sense them as well.

"It's Finn and Uncle Andrew," she said aloud as she identified Marius and Pollux. "They're supposed to be farther up the line," she added, mostly to herself.

"What's that?" the man asked sharply.

"Two more riders are coming," Anthea told him. "From relay stations farther up the road." She frowned. "One of them is the leader of the Horse Brigade, Captain Andrew Thornley."

"Thornley?" the man said, looking even more pale. "Then we are at war."

2

THE LAST CAMP

LEONIDAS CAME OVER TO the paddock ropes as Anthea slid off Florian's back. The nearly black stallion radiated concern, his broad chest pressing against the makeshift fence.

It had taken hours for Anthea and the others to reach the brigade's camp, since Arthur Watson refused to touch or ride on a horse, and Leonidas had been pacing and snorting since Anthea had reached out to him to say that she was near. He had only gone to this camp with Brutus and Caillin Mac-Rennie because Anthea had promised that she would follow in two days' time, and it had been three days, as he was quick to inform her.

Leonidas had recovered from his injuries after being caught in a snare months ago, but the whole episode had made him very anxious. Mostly he wanted to prove himself to Anthea, over and over again, to show that he was sorry.

Because he had run away, he had gotten caught in the snare. Because he had run away, Anthea had been shot and then become ill. Because he had run away, the mare Bluebell had also been hurt. Because of *him*.

"Shall I ride you later, to stretch your legs, Leonidas?" Anthea fondly tugged his forelock with one hand as she pulled Florian's reins around with the other.

Please, Beloved of Florian, Leonidas said. *I was worried that you were hurt*, he said after a pause.

She was with me, Florian reminded him.

Leonidas shied away. Anthea gave Florian a mental reprimand and reached out to slap Leonidas on the shoulder. Gently.

I am quite well, Leonidas. Thank you! Only we had to bring a stranger with us, and he would not ride, she explained. *Then I took my message to the next courier.*

She did not add that he had not yet left with it. No one was leaving the camp, not with Andrew and Finn just arriving, and without a word to anyone about why they had left their posts.

Florian lowered his ears. He did not like these developments, but even more, he did not like Arthur Watson. None of the horses liked strangers, and when Anthea had arrived with Uncle Andrew and Finn and another man who insisted on walking to the side of the horses, there had been quite a hue and cry. Watson had quickly been ushered into the command tent and Anthea had herded Marius and Pollux into a paddock, even before uselessly passing along her message to the rider who was supposed to carry it on.

He Who Will Walk smells of fear, Florian said, using the name that he had come up with for Arthur Watson.

I know, my darling, Anthea replied through the Way. She sighed. *They always do.*

Anthea patted Florian and tied him to the nearest post. She would need to take off his tack and brush him down before she turned him in to the paddock, but first she wanted to know what was happening in that tent.

She lifted the tent flap and stepped inside. It was dim, after the bright morning light in the clearing, and Anthea was embarrassed by the squeaking noise she made as she first collided with Watson and then stumbled the rest of the way into the tent. Anthea managed to grab the edge of a folding table to keep from falling.

"Whoa! Careful there!"

Andrew caught Anthea's arm before she could put her hand in an open bottle of ink. She muttered an apology and he gave her elbow a squeeze as she righted herself.

"I believe you've met Mr. Watson," he said.

"Yes." She nodded at him. "My name is Anthea Thornley," she added, since they hadn't been properly introduced. "Courier First Class. Of the Horse Brigade."

Everyone just looked at one another. So Anthea went ahead and asked it.

"The Crown sent you to photograph what, exactly?"

It wasn't the only question she wanted to ask. The other question, one she wanted to ask even more urgently, was what he had meant when he said they were at war. But she thought it was probably better to ease into that.

"The horses, and the men," Watson said. Then he looked at Anthea. "I mean, and women, er . . . everyone." He finished in a rush. "The Crown has sent me to photograph you. All."

Anthea felt her scarred eyebrow lifting. She looked across the table to Caillin MacRennie, who also looked skeptical. He was sewing a button back on his own coat, but he kept watching Watson while he sewed without looking down, which was disconcerting.

"The Crown? Or the king?" Caillin MacRennie asked.

Growing up, Anthea had always thought of the Crown as being a single entity, with the king as the head and everyone from the queen to the lowliest courtier as the body, all working in harmony.

Now that the brigade actually worked for the king and the queen—and there were rumors that the royal advisors were doing their utmost to get the brigade exiled and Andrew arrested for treason—they knew differently. The brigade had been the queen's idea, one that the king had gone along with only reluctantly. The queen was of an old horse-loving Leanan family, something that the king did not like to talk about. What he did like to talk about was how he would get rid of the brigade the moment they didn't prove themselves useful.

"But tell them what you said on the road," Anthea prompted the photographer when it looked like he wasn't going to say anything more. He opened his mouth and she cut him off. "*Not* about photographs, the other thing you said, when you heard that Uncle Andrew and the others had left their stations."

Watson looked around helplessly. Since the brigade wasn't really part of the army, the riders didn't have any official insignia. Everyone in the tent had an army issue coat, but there was no indication of rank. Beside which: Anthea was a girl, and Finn was only a year older than Anthea. Andrew was in his forties, but he looked much younger despite the little gray in his hair. He was wearing a cable-knit sweater and had thrown his coat over a stool in the corner. He was marking something on the map spread across the table as though he couldn't be bothered to give a visitor his full attention. Caillin MacRennie was the oldest person in the tent, and he was also coatless, sitting on a barrel.

The confused photographer finally directed his eyes to the back of the tent and held out a letter to anyone who would take it.

"The Crown sent me," he said again, to no one in particular. "That's all I know."

Uncle Andrew took the letter, looking amused.

"Have a seat," he said, pointing vaguely to the various collapsible stools around the table as he slit the heavy wax seal with a pocketknife.

"Is it from *His* Majesty, or *Her* Majesty?" Caillin MacRennie asked. He bit off a thread and shook out his coat.

Watson gasped. "It's from the *Crown*," he said.

"Yes, well, we actually know what that means," Finn said.

Watson gasped again, but this time he was looking at something. Anthea turned.

Jilly had just arrived. Of course Arthur Watson had gasped.

Anthea's gray army overcoat was warm and serviceable. Both girls had been given the two smallest ones Andrew could find when they were outfitting the riders. But the smallest size made to fit a grown soldier was still slightly too big for the cousins. And Jilly did not like wearing anything that was bulky. Or plain.

She had tailored the coat so closely to her figure that Anthea marveled Jilly could fit a shirt underneath, and replaced the standard-issue black leather-covered buttons with blue velvet ones. And that was just to start with. In the evenings, Jilly embroidered an expanding pattern of vines and horse heads around the hem and up the sleeves, in blue and red and green, and today she had accessorized with a blue silk scarf tied around her jaunty curls.

Jilly was just generally striking. She was, in fact, turning into a great beauty. Meanwhile, Anthea was frequently mistaken for "one of the men" until people noticed her long hair. But Anthea shoved her jealousy aside.

"How long did it take you to get here?" Jilly demanded as

she dropped the tent flap behind her and kissed her father on the cheek and then gave Anthea a hug. She was clearly bursting to tell them her time, her cheeks rosy and her eyes bright. Outside, Anthea sensed Caesar and Florian greeting each other, as fond of each other as their riders were.

"Six hours," Anthea said shortly. "And then some."

"Four and a half!" Jilly crowed, before Anthea had even finished.

"The mist was terrible, and then this happened," Anthea said, jerking her head at the photographer.

"Yes, who *are* you?"

The shocked look on the photographer's face, which had been in danger of turning to a gooey-eyed expression, was wiped clean by this. Despite her generally flighty air and penchant for unique fashions, Jilly was indeed her father's daughter. And her father was the commander of the Horse Brigade.

"Have you shown them your credentials?" Jilly asked. "How did you find us?"

"He's not a new recruit," Anthea said. "He's a photographer."

"What? Why?" Jilly frowned at the man, who wilted.

"The—the king sent me?"

"Hmm," Jilly said.

"My name is Arthur Watson," the photographer said.

"She has a pet owl named Arthur," Jilly informed him, waving a hand at Anthea. "So we'll just call you Watson."

"Er, all right . . . ?"

"You said we were at war," Anthea said loudly.

"There's always rumors of war," Caillin MacRennie said soothingly.

"The Kronenhofer emperor has been threatening to withdraw all trade unless we—" Finn began.

"The Kronenhofer emperor has been threatening to withdraw trade for years," Caillin MacRennie said. He started to say something else, but then he frowned. "Is that why you came all the way here, Andrew? Or was there something else?"

Andrew cleared his throat. "We got word from our . . . patron . . . that we needed to consolidate our forces, and possibly send some of our younger riders back to Leana."

"And I don't think we need to panic," Finn interjected. "The qu—our patron, that is, didn't say why, just that there were rumors of trouble."

"Actually, sir?" Watson raised his hand. He looked at Andrew, seeming a little relieved to identify the man in charge.

"Yes?"

"Two Kronenhofer naval ships came up the river toward Coronam last week. They refused to dock or reply to any signals. When one of our river patrol boats tried to approach, they fired on it. I think what this patron of yours is trying to say is . . . well, now we *are* at war with Kronenhof."

3

PHOTOGRAPHS

"NO, PULL THE ANIMAL'S head down. Farther. Will it bite you?"

Florian heaved a sigh. Anthea echoed it.

"He won't bite," Anthea said, trying for patience as she shortened the reins again so that Florian's head was hanging right over her shoulder. "He's not a wild dog."

"Oh. All right."

Watson ducked under the black cloth that hung from the square box of his camera. Anthea held as still as she could, sending thoughts of calmness and steadiness to Florian as she did. He didn't need them: he was intrigued by the idea of the camera and eager to have his picture taken.

"Now his head is covering too much of your, um, coat," Watson said.

Anthea sighed again. Jilly had tried to get Anthea to wear her tailored and embroidered coat, but Anthea had refused. She had always thought that photographs were strange. People dressed up in clothes that they would never normally wear, their hair in stiff styles that forced them to hold their heads at unnatural angles. Watson was here to take pictures of the Horse Brigade for historical record. Not a fairy tale, but a real accounting of them, and so Anthea wanted to look like herself.

She wore her best trousers, and had her boots polished to a shine. Jilly had retaliated by pinning the back of Anthea's coat so that it was more fitted and fell open to show that Anthea wore one of her favorite middy blouses underneath, of which Jilly actually approved.

"I don't recognize you without your sailor suits," she had joked as she did Anthea's hair.

Anthea's hair was the other thing they both agreed on. Jilly had carefully twisted Anthea's long wavy tresses into curls and then pomaded them so that they would stay, then she pulled them to the side and tied them with a red ribbon under Anthea's right ear. Anthea wore the silver rose earrings that the queen had given her for her birthday last month, and pinned the silver rose pendant her aunt Deirdre (a former Rose Maiden to the queen) had given her next to the silver horseshoe charm from her late father on the lapel of her coat.

Of course the red ribbon wouldn't show up in the

black-and-white picture, and now Florian's head was covering her jewelry. The photographer had him standing straight on, with his head hanging over her shoulder and her hand gripping the reins.

"No, no, no," Finn said, coming out of his tent and seeing what was happening.

"That's terrible. You can't see Florian or Thea, so what's the point?"

"Are you a photographer?" Watson snapped.

"No, but I have eyes," Finn retorted.

Florian snorted. Anthea snickered in her throat, still trying not to move.

"Here," Finn said.

He took the reins from Anthea and moved Florian around so that the horse was standing behind Anthea, her against the saddle. Finn put the reins back in Anthea's right hand, and gently moved Florian so that his neck was curved around and his head was next to Anthea's shoulder but not hanging over it. Finn then arranged Anthea's hair, to her embarrassment, turning the curls so that they hung nicely and adjusting the ribbon so that the bow was straight.

Finn was standing very close to her to do it. She could feel his breath stirring the tendrils of escaped hair on her forehead. He smiled down at her and then cleared his throat.

"You should let Jilly fix your coat permanently," he said in a low voice.

"I—I can't get it buttoned like this," she muttered, feeling her cheeks burn.

"Oh," Finn said.

Anthea glanced up and saw that now Finn was blushing, too. He stepped back.

"There, try that," he said to Watson. "Now you can actually see both of them."

"I'll have to move the camera back," Watson said.

"Then do it," Finn said shortly.

Fussing and muttering, Watson moved his tripod back a few inches and then disappeared under the cloth. Anthea and Florian both sighed but didn't move until he replaced the cap.

"All right," Watson said. "Who's next?"

Anthea started to lead Florian away.

"Wait," Finn said. "Let me bring out some of the others and we can all have a picture together. Keth is ready, and hopefully Jilly is done beautifying herself. Let's have a picture of the four us," Finn said.

"I will never be done, because I am worth waiting for," Jilly announced, coming out of the tent she shared with Anthea.

Watson wasn't the only one gaping.

She had smoothed and shined her light brown curls so that they made a halo around her face. She had pinned her own rose (a gift from the queen) and a horseshoe charm from Uncle Andrew to her lapel, along with an emerald brooch that was so large it looked fake (though knowing Jilly, it was likely very real). She was wearing a tightly fitted silk blouse and a blue-and-pink paisley ascot, riding breeches that looked painted on, and boots so glossy you could see your reflection in them.

As usual, Anthea instantly felt grubby and younger than her years. Jilly, eyes twinkling, pulled a ruby brooch out of her pocket, pinned it to Anthea's lapel, and grinned at her. Then she reached into her other pocket and pulled out Arthur, setting him on Anthea's right shoulder so that he wouldn't hide in her hair.

"You look gorgeous," Jilly said. "Are you sure you won't let me fix your coat like this permanently?"

"Finn asked the same thing," Anthea whispered.

"Did he, now?" Jilly waggled her eyebrows, and Anthea found herself blushing again. "I'm going to get Caesar and Buttercup, because it's only fair. Do you want me to bring Bluebell and Leonidas, too?"

"Let's see how many horses we can get in the picture," Keth said with a laugh. His laugh turned into a cough. "Woof! Excuse me," he said.

Keth was the fourth of the young people, a half-Leanan, half-Kadiji boy whose mother was the brigade's beloved Nurse Shannon. He had come back from a courier mission to Travertine just in time to join the mock war that morning.

"And how was the big mission, by the way?" Anthea asked as they waited for Finn to arrange the horses, while Watson paced back and forth, wringing his hands.

"Boring," Keth said.

"I'm sorry, did *you* just spend the last month standing in some mist and looking at nothing?" Anthea demanded.

"Well, no," Keth laughed. "But I did spend it sitting around an army barracks, having people whisper about me, and occasionally passing on messages. Not even important messages, you know, but random words and things."

"I know," Anthea sighed. "All the messages were coded that way."

"And I never thought I'd say this," Keth said. "But passing messages through the Way was boring!"

Sometimes they were close enough to send the message directly through the Way, sometimes they had to ride closer to reach. It depended on the rider, and the horse, and the strength of their bond. And while being close enough to pass a message through the Way made Anthea feel proud, she also had to admit that just standing there thinking "teapot caterpillar dragon florist" was not half as exciting as galloping down the highway to deliver the message in person.

"I know," she sighed again.

"So boring," Keth agreed.

He stroked Gaius Julius's nose and stepped in close to Anthea. Finn brought Anthea's two other charges: Leonidas and the gray mare Bluebell. She had Florian hanging over her right shoulder, so Arthur flapped up to sit between his ears, wrapping his claws around the headstall of Florian's bridle.

Beyond Keth, Jilly was fussing around rearranging Caesar and her mare Buttercup, and wondering aloud if they should have put flowers or ribbons in the mares' manes to show that they were female.

"I want to sleep," Keth said. "Please can we do this so that I can go sleep?"

"Not yet," Andrew said, coming out of his tent. He looked at the arrangement and then, to Watson's evident annoyance, he said, "Good, good, perfect.

"Then we will see how many of the men we can fit into a picture. We need plenty of photographs, and always with at least one horse in them."

"The Crown ordered me to take a *few* photographs—" Watson began.

"The letter you gave me said that I was to dictate how many photographs you took and who they were to be of," Andrew said, cutting him off. "And I want as many as possible. And always with a horse in them."

"We can get more men in the picture if the animals aren't there."

Andrew looked him square in the face. "I want to make it very hard to erase the Horse Brigade, when the king eventually tires of us."

"I don't know what you're . . . I'm not sure I can—" Watson spluttered, but Andrew cut him off again.

"You can and you will," Andrew said. "Or we'll have the

queen here in a matter of days." He paused. "She keeps horses, too, you know," he added, making it sound like a threat.

Anthea couldn't tell if Watson did know, or if he was just intimidated by Andrew, but it worked either way. He kept on taking pictures until the light began to fade, only speaking to tell someone to hold still or move in closer.

And all while this was happening, Anthea and the other riders with the Way were carrying on a lengthy conversation through their horses about Kronenhof and the impending war.

What is an act of aggression? Florian wanted to know when they were done. *How is sailing on a boat a thing that becomes a war?*

I don't really understand it either, Anthea confessed as she finally let him loose in the paddock. He stayed nearby, however, his ears back with concern. *But they are not supposed to have boats like that, boats with guns on them, in our rivers.*

And now everyone must fight?

Apparently, my love.

But would the king ask the Horse Brigade to fight? The king didn't trust them to carry messages more secret than "blue triangle teacup" or "Today in Bellair it rained for one hour."

We should be allowed to take our place in the army, Finn said via Marius, as though he had read her thoughts.

Caesar and I are ready to fight, Jilly said through Caesar, baring her teeth in a devil-may-care smile.

I'll be offended if we aren't allowed to fight, Anthea said. *But I'm terrified at the idea all the same!*

We still don't know what's happening for certain, Brutus said, on behalf of Caillin MacRennie.

"Well, if we need to know," Jilly said aloud as they finished up the last photograph, "there's clearly only one thing to do!"

She looked at Anthea, as though expecting her to finish the thought, but Anthea just blinked in confusion. Watson stopped putting away his camera to look at her. Jilly did have a very carrying voice. Everyone stopped to look at her. She threw an arm around Anthea as though they were having another picture done.

"Anthea and I will just go visit our dear friend the queen, and find out for sure if we're going to war!"

CONSTANTINE

Useless human fillies. They had caused no end of trouble.

He could hear them talking now, talking and talking to his rider. They would take his rider away with them, on that inferior stallion, that one who dared to carry the Rider of the Herd Stallion. They would take his rider, and leave him behind. They would take other stallions, and mares, dividing the herd. That one, that Florian, that one who had dared to step into Constantine's private field, that one who had dared to protect the girl when she needed punishment, he would get above his place.

There was only one herd stallion. Constantine.

It did not matter how far they traveled, how many days. The men thought they could say, You, horse, in this place, you are herd stallion. They said it to Florian. They said it to Marius, who dared to carry his rider. They said it to Brutus.

No.

There was only Constantine.

Now these weak and foolish girls were talking, talking, talking of kings of men who were not his rider. Useless. They would go away, Constantine wanted them to go away. But they would take his mares. They would make Florian a herd stallion, which they had no power to do.

Constantine rose to his hind legs. He screamed his rage. As his front hooves came down, he easily destroyed the fence on one side of his paddock. The men rushed to repair it and to soothe him. But he would not be soothed. They must listen to him: he was herd stallion. His rider was the one and only king.

They must listen.

4

TEA AT BELL HYDE

"REALLY, DEAR, I WOULD be happy to take a look at that coat," Queen Josephine said as they settled down to tea.

"But I like my coat," Anthea protested weakly. "Doesn't anyone else . . . ?"

Jilly twinkled at her over the rim of her teacup. Princess Margaret, who was only a couple of years younger than Anthea, looked around, confused. Then she saw how Jilly was sitting and also crossed her legs right over left, to copy her. The queen smiled and reached over the tiny table to pat Anthea's hand.

"If you like it, I like it," Queen Josephine said. "I just wondered if you'd like something that fits a bit better. I know you are supposed to wear a uniform because you're part of the army, but the army just isn't equipped to . . . equip girls!" She dunked a scone in her tea and took a big bite, still smiling.

"Thank you, but I'm not that concerned about my coat," Anthea said. "I'm more worried about going to war."

"Yes, I thought that might be why you came," the queen said. She sighed and put down her half-eaten scone. She jutted her chin at Margaret.

The princess hurried to the door of the sitting room where they were having tea. She looked into the entrance hall, said something in a low voice to the guard there, and then closed the tall double doors. She took her place next to Jilly and nodded to her mother.

"We are going to do everything possible to avoid a war," the queen said in a low, rapid voice. "What happened on the Crown River last week was terrible. My husband's people are still looking into it. We don't know who sent those ships, and we do not know who gave the order to open fire from either side. There is a great deal of shrugging, and messages going awry, but no one will claim responsibility."

"What?" Anthea almost dropped her cup. "None of the brigade's messages, I hope!"

"No," the queen said, her brow creased. "None of yours . . ."

"We could take a message to the Kronenhofer king," Jilly said eagerly.

"We could?" Anthea said in alarm.

Fortunately Princess Margaret was already shaking her head. "Father will never agree to that," she said. "He just found out that I'm learning to ride, and I thought actual steam would come out of his ears!"

"But your mother rides," Jilly said in disbelief. "The queen!" She pointed to Queen Josephine, as though the others didn't know whom she meant.

"My husband learned long ago to give me my way in some things," the queen said with a small smile. "But—"

"He still thinks he should have total control over his children," Margaret said bitterly.

Anthea played with her teaspoon and took another scone even though she hadn't eaten her first. "Do you have the Way?" she asked in a rush.

She was never sure if it was a rude thing to ask or not. Jilly, who had only recently developed it (which was rare), had been very sensitive about it until lately. Out of the corner of her eye, Anthea saw Jilly lean forward eagerly, and guessed that it was all right to ask.

"I—I think I might," Princess Margaret said. She licked her lips, nervous. "I thought that I could smell something like oats or hay that I couldn't have smelled from that part of the field, the last time I tried to ride. And . . . and I thought I could feel happiness from Blossom, but that might have been, might have been wishful thinking, you know?"

"My darling, that's wonderful!" Queen Josephine put out her hand and squeezed her daughter's.

"That is how it starts," Jilly said sagely. "I'm only just now, after being around horses all my life, able to use real words with them."

"It was the same for me," the queen said. "First the scents, and then emotions, and now I get words, but only from Holly."

All three of them looked expectantly at Anthea. She looked down at her tea, uncomfortable.

"I, er, don't remember anything from when I was little," she admitted. "And then they brought me back to the farm last year, and I, er, just suddenly felt all the horses and . . . smelled things . . . and . . . knew things that the horses knew."

She had, in fact, rescued Jilly's beloved Caesar within a few hours of arriving. Caesar had eaten a sponge, and Anthea had known instantly what was causing him distress. But from the moment that the farm's ancient motorcar had pulled through the gates, Anthea had heard and smelled and felt what all the horses were thinking and smelling and feeling. It wasn't until she had rediscovered Florian that she had been able to calm down and focus the Way to shut out the rest of the noise.

Everyone was still looking at her. Jilly sighed loudly. Margaret looked sad. Self-conscious, Anthea took a too large bite of one of her scones and nearly choked as Caesar had. Jilly helpfully moved over to the sofa beside Anthea and thumped her repeatedly on the back.

"Perhaps I don't have the Way after all," Margaret said.

"I'm sure you do," Jilly said. "It's just that Anthea is a prodigy."

"I am not," Anthea protested faintly.

"Of course you are, dear," Queen Josephine said. "And there's nothing wrong with that."

"I don't know how much of it is me, though," Anthea said. "And how much of it is because my father, well, *experimented* on me."

Princess Margaret gasped. "And I thought my father was bad!" she said when they all looked at her.

"Oh, no, I mean, my father loved me," Anthea scrambled to explain. Her cheeks burned as she realized what she'd said. "And I'm sure your father, the king, loves you very much, too. But he, er, with Florian, there was something."

Jilly, who was calmly sipping her tea and watching Anthea with great amusement, finally came to her rescue. "My uncle Charles, Anthea's late father, had a theory that the Way would be stronger if the horse and the rider were brought together at a much younger age," she said demurely. "He had Anthea be present at Florian's birth, had her feed him by hand as much as possible, and care for him, even though she was hardly more than a baby.

"And he was clearly right."

"Fascinating," the queen said, giving Anthea a look of great admiration. "But there's no need for the rest of us to despair," she added, turning to pat her daughter's hand. "Jilly lives with horses and only just developed the Way in the last year."

"When the king isn't here, spend as much time with the horses as you can," Jilly urged the princess. "If your father says not to ride them, that's not ideal, but can you not visit them in their pasture? Pet them? Groom them?"

"I—I suppose I could do that," Margaret said. "I mean, I have been doing that," she clarified with more confidence.

"Leave your father to me, Meg," Queen Josephine said. "In light of this issue with the Kronenhofer ships, he will surely want to have as many people with the Way working for him as possible."

"What *is* this issue with the Kronenhofer ships?" Anthea asked, glad to not have any more talk about experiments or her being a prodigy. "You said no one was sure what had happened?"

"It is all very odd, and you may speak of it only to Captain Thornley," the queen said. "Oh, and Finn, of course." Unlike her husband, Queen Josephine had no problem recognizing Finn as a descendant of kings.

"So all that we know," Queen Josephine continued, "is that two warships appeared quite suddenly at the mouth of the Crown River. There was no record of them requesting passage down the river, which means that it was a hostile act.

"But of course our river guard approached them in one of their small boats, and hailed the lead ship, to ask their intent. But they didn't get an answer. Instead, the ship went into battle mode: all the portholes were locked up and the guns were moved into position to fire on the river guard.

"The river guard gave another warning, and there was

still no response, so they signaled to the garrison on shore, they fired a warning shot, and then the Kronenhofer ships opened fire. They turned the river guard ship into kindling and began to fire on the garrison. The garrison disabled the Kronenhofer ships. One of them sank, and the other burned almost to the waterline, and there were only a handful of survivors."

"And what did they say?" Anthea asked breathlessly. "Why did they come?"

"Unfortunately, none of the survivors are very high ranking officers. All they were told was that they were to come to Coronam to discuss a great insult that was given to their emperor by my husband. But none of them knew what it was.

"And letters that have been sent to Emperor Otto have just gotten a response, which is that he has no idea what those ships were doing there, that he knows of no insult, and did not order them to sail."

"But *now* he's insulted," Princess Margaret said, her voice grim. "And very, very angry that two of his newest ships are gone."

"It couldn't have happened at a worse time," Queen Josephine said with a sigh. "There's been a great deal of arguments about trade agreements that are expiring this year," she explained. "All very boring, but necessary, and then when something like this happens, it just adds a strain that makes things more complicated."

"It sounds like someone did it on purpose," Jilly mused.

"Oh, I don't think—" the queen began, but then someone knocked softly on the double doors and entered.

It was a maid in a crisp blue gown with a white apron. She bobbed a curtsey.

"I beg your pardon, Your Majesty, but it's time to dress for dinner."

"The doors were *closed*," Margaret said, under her breath.

"Ah, thank you, Anne," the queen said, shooting her daughter a quelling look. "But just for future reference, if the doors are closed, please just knock and someone will come out."

The maid turned slowly red.

"It's quite all right," the queen said, rising. "You couldn't have known. But where is Daphne? She's usually the one trying to keep me on schedule." The queen laughed and shook her head at Jilly and Anthea.

"Isn't this her week to visit her family?" Princess Margaret said, standing and brushing crumbs off her skirt.

Anthea was glad to see she wasn't the only one who had enjoyed her scones literally to pieces.

"Ah, yes, she's still in Travertine, then," the queen said. She turned to Jilly and Anthea. "Well, you'll join us for dinner, of course?

"Meg, dear, will you get them some of your sister's gowns? I'm guessing they only brought what could fit in a saddlebag."

"Oh, Annabel has just the thing. Things," Margaret said,

eyes lighting up. "I'm not allowed to wear them. But *you* could."

"Begging your pardon again, Your Majesty," Anne said as they passed her going out of the sitting room. "But Daphne . . . she's back from Tra'tine."

"Oh, is she?" Queen Josephine looked at the maid. "How odd! I haven't seen her. Did she just get back this afternoon?"

"She got back two days ago," Anne said, her voice trembling. "But she, she's real sick, Your Majesty. I wasn't supposed to say anything unless she was still sick tomorrow, Mrs. Hodges said not to. But Daphne's my best friend, ma'am, and . . . can't we call the doctor today?"

The queen put a hand on the girl's thin shoulder. "Yes, yes, we can! But first, dear, you'd better take me to Daphne!"

FLORIAN

Florian did not like this place. The queen of men, Beloved of Holly, was kind and smelled always of good things. The house was always full of kind people, and there were many girls who liked to bring treats to the horses. It was good to see the mares he had known, too. Holly and Juniper, Blossom and Campanula were familiar to him from the Last Farm, as well as Domitian, who had been brought to this place to be their herd stallion, even though he had many years.

But Florian did not like the big stone house where Beloved Anthea would disappear for many hours at a time. The first time they had come to this place, she had been very sick, too sick to ride him or visit him, but the Soon King had kept them in a paddock right outside the windows. He had left many of the windows open, in all weather, so that the horses could see him and he could speak to them often.

But now other men, men who did not understand such matters, had built a paddock, away from the house. They had built a stable, and it was very nice, warm and dry. But Florian could not see the window where Beloved Anthea slept. If he called to her with his voice, she could not hear him, and if he called to her with the Way, it took her too long to leave the stone house and come to him.

And Florian did not like the scents here. There was the scent of that king of men, that mate of Beloved of Holly who was loud and smelled of anger and fear, who would not touch a horse or look on them with kindness. He was not here, but his scent lingered and he might return at any time. Another smell was present, too, a smell that slid into Florian's nostrils and brought fear with it. Florian thought he had smelled it at the camp, when the man with the box had made their pictures, but he wasn't sure. Now he smelled it strongly, and he was sure, and he did not like it.

It was a rank, creeping smell. A smell of sickness.

We must go, he called out to Beloved Anthea.

Soon, she answered. Soon.

Florian paced the paddock and looked at his companions.

We must go, he said to them. There is sickness.

If you can smell it, Domitian said. It is too late.

5

ON THE ROAD

"ARE WE BEING EXILED?" Jilly said suddenly. She turned in her saddle to look at Anthea. Jilly looked delighted at the idea, her blue eyes sparkling.

"No," Anthea said, horrified. "Of course not!"

She drew Florian alongside Caesar so that Jilly wouldn't need to shout to be heard. Especially if she was going to shout things like *that*. They were plodding up the main highway to the north, having just met up with two dozen more of the brigade who were leaving their courier posts and going back to Last Farm.

"Oh, come on! We *are* being sent beyond the Wall," Jilly said, eyes gleaming. "Just like the exiles of old! Can't we say we've been exiled?"

"We're not being *sent* beyond the Wall, we *live* beyond the

Wall," Anthea said, exasperated. "We're not being exiled . . . Why would you want that?"

"It makes us sound dangerous and exciting," Keth said, coming up on Jilly's other side. "Pardon me, miss," he intoned. "Could you give a lonely exile directions?" His flirtatious air was marred by a sudden hacking cough that started on the last word and kept going for a full five minutes while he huddled over his stallion's neck.

"Do you *still* have that cough?" Jilly asked when he was done.

"First of all," he gasped. "*Yes*, obviously. And secondly, does it offend your ladyship or something?"

"No, I mean, I didn't mean to," Jilly said, flustered. "Sound that way. I meant, poor you . . ."

"I'm sure she didn't mean to sound accusatory," Anthea chimed in. "But really, that's a horrible cough! Are you all right?"

"Just caught something riding back and forth and sleeping in tents for the last month," Keth said with a shrug. He coughed again.

"What did Nurse Shannon say?"

He smells all right to me, Florian interjected. Anthea stroked his neck.

"She said that as a nurse she thinks I'm fine," Keth said. "But as a mother she wants me to go home and get plenty of rest." He shrugged. "So here I go!"

"She wants her own son to be exiled?" Jilly put the back of her gloved hand to her brow. "Tragic!"

"We are *not* being exiled," Anthea scolded, looking around to see if there was anyone nearby.

She wasn't worried about any of the other riders hearing them. They were used to Jilly's theatrics, and some of them actually *were* exiles, though Anthea had never dared to ask which riders, or why. She didn't want to find out that the grandfatherly man who carved little wooden horses for her, or the gruff but kindly one who offered to clean her saddle, were murderers.

There were about twenty riders, including Anthea, Jilly, and Keth, and twice that many horses heading back to the farm. They were to wait there for instructions about a new system of passing messages that the king was working on with Andrew's help. What Anthea worried about was passing some people who weren't riders and having them think they were some sort of dreadful mass exiling.

"Does it actually matter?" Jilly said when she saw Anthea standing in her stirrups to try and look over a hedgerow.

"Yes, it does," Anthea said.

"You know if you want to be a Rose Maiden, you can just ask the queen in person to make you one? And she probably will," Jilly said.

Once upon a time Anthea's fondest wish had been to be one of the queen's elite ladies-in-waiting. The Rose Maidens were held up as the finest, most accomplished women in all Coronam. Her mother had been one, and Anthea had thought that her mother's career had ended with her untimely death. However, it turned out that her mother had *not* died, but had abandoned Anthea and gone on to be one of the king's most trusted spies.

Meeting her mother at long last, and finding out about Genevia Cross-Thornley's rather sinister career, had initially cured Anthea of any desire to be a Rose Maiden. But after getting to know Queen Josephine, Anthea had begun to think that if she could be a Rose Maiden, and still be with Florian, it might be all right. There had never been a Leanan horsewoman who was also a Rose Maiden, and Anthea was secretly thrilled at the idea of being the first.

"It's not that," Anthea said, blushing to think how it would have been exactly that not too long ago. "But do you think that people will want to make friends with the horses and receive messages from their riders if they believe that we're all exiles?"

"She has a point," Keth said. "Especially since some of us are children."

"*I'm* not a child," Jilly argued, then stopped. "Which I guess makes it worse."

"No one here is an exile," Rogers, the rider in charge of the group, dropped back to say. "And since we are about to turn into that farmyard and ask to water our horses, I would appreciate it if you would change the subject!"

"I suppose," Jilly said, giving a pained sigh. "Though I don't know why you have to rob us of our one pleasure on this dreary march toward our exile."

Rogers looked helplessly at Anthea.

"I'll stuff my handkerchief in her mouth," Anthea told him.

"Thank you, Miss Thea," he said.

He urged his stallion to the front of the group as they turned down a short lane that led to a farmhouse and out-buildings. The other riders drew their horses into ranks behind him, putting the strings of riderless horses in the middle. Anthea was leading her two charges, Leonidas and Bluebell, and she gave their leading line a tug so that Bluebell was right next to Florian and Leonidas just behind. He started to crowd Florian, who laid his ears back, so Anthea turned in the saddle and gave the other stallion a dire look along with a mental warning, and he dropped back. Bluebell complained about the stallions jostling her, and Anthea reached over and rubbed the mare's neck as she reassured her with the Way.

Jilly moved her horses back and around so that Buttercup was beside Bluebell, the two mares greeting each other with flickering ears and little whickers, and Caesar was on the other side of them. Buttercup and Bluebell, long-time herd-mates, were the first horses that Jilly or Anthea had ridden, and Anthea often felt guilty that so much of her time in the saddle was now spent on Florian.

Anthea had to remind herself that it was actually Florian she had ridden first, sitting on his back as a small child, her father holding her in place so that they would have a feel for each other. She had no memories of this, but Florian had shared his impression with her, so she had some strange images from time to time, almost as if she had once been a horse. She had tentatively asked her uncle if such a thing was possible, and he had reassured her that she had been born human, and would stay human, though he did sound a little wistful about it.

Anthea felt the jealousy coming from Leonidas and turned around again, this time to assure him that he was being very, very good, and she also loved him. She did it entirely through the Way, however, without adding any patting or tugs at his mane, since they were now drawing up in the farmyard, near the well, scattering chickens and geese as they did so. A black-and-white collie dog came out to bark at them, but the tabby cat lounging on the side of the well barely looked up before returning to grooming her paws.

The combination of the collie barking and the commotion that resulted from dozens of hooves stamping on hard-packed dirt brought the farmwife running. She stopped short in the doorway, apron clenched in her fists and dishcloth forgotten on one shoulder. After goggling for a full minute, she yelled at the dog.

"Jyp! Get in here!" There was a rising note of panic in her voice.

"Excuse me, ma'am," Rogers called out to her. "Please don't be alarmed! We need your help!"

The woman grabbed the dog by the collar and started to drag him into the house, never taking her eyes off the nearest horse, and Anthea didn't blame her. The nearest horse was Rogers's stallion, which was very tall and imposing.

"Hold them," Anthea said, handing Jilly the leads for Bluebell and Leonidas.

She nudged Florian with her mind and he edged forward through the herd until they were at the front. Luckily the farmwife hadn't been able to close the door yet; the dog was trying to make sure that the horses knew exactly whose farm they were invading.

"Good afternoon," Anthea called out over the barking. "Ma'am? Can you help us please?"

The woman's eyes slowly took in Anthea's long hair hanging over her shoulder, the high-necked, pleated front of her white blouse under her army coat, and then the rose pinned to her lapel. The farmwife made a perfect O with her mouth and then, grasping the dog firmly by the collar to make sure he didn't get free, she stepped back out of the house and closed the door behind her.

"Are you . . . are you a Rose Maiden?"

My Own Jilly says to say yes, came from Caesar.

"We are friends of the queen," Anthea said primly.

"Under orders from the Crown," Rogers threw in, but he had moved aside to give Anthea more room.

"Friends of the queen?" the woman said, her eyes narrowing.

"Yes, ma'am," Anthea said. "Well, my cousin and I are." She waved a hand over her shoulder in Jilly's general direction. "But all of the horses and their riders work for the Crown. We're called the Horse Brigade."

My Own Jilly says stop talking, you are being awkward.

Tell your own Jilly she isn't helping, Anthea shot back.

"I see," the farmwife said. "And why are you here?"

"We need water," Anthea said. "Could we draw from your well to water our horses?"

The woman's expression went from astonishment to horror in less than a heartbeat. She raised her arms as though to sweep them all up, letting go of the dog, who ran in the midst of the horses' legs, making noises that were not quite barks now that he saw how big the intruders were.

"Stay away from my water!" the woman cried out.

Rogers looked just as horrified, and started to back his horse away. The combination of her shrill voice and the dog dancing around their feet was making all the horses stamp and whicker nervously. Anthea and the other riders hurried to tell them to hold still: the last thing they needed was for the horses to go into a panic and trample the dog or run into a field and ruin the crops.

The woman put one hand over her nose and mouth and waved frantically at the horses with the other, shooing them away. She hurried over to the well to block it with her body.

And then Anthea realized why the woman was so upset. It

would have been the same reaction she herself would have had a year ago.

"They're not diseased," Anthea shouted at the woman, over the muted barking and the woman's cries and Rogers's huffing and puffing. "The horses, they don't have any diseases!"

Rogers, born and raised north of Kalabar's Wall, turned and looked at Anthea in complete bafflement. The woman, however, turned and looked with a mingling of surprise and suspicion.

"It's true," Anthea said. "Hundreds of years ago many people and horses died of a disease that is long gone, I promise. All of our horses are healthy. You can't get sick from them."

Light dawned on Rogers's face. "We have our own buckets," he announced. "We can use our own buckets!"

The brigade was fully equipped with camping gear, including things that Anthea had never known existed. Among these were collapsible leather buckets that fit very nicely into saddlebags.

"Like this!" Jilly called out.

Anthea turned in her saddle to see that her cousin had already snatched her bucket from a saddlebag and snapped it out to demonstrate it. The other riders quickly began finding theirs. From the muttered curses, some of them had not bothered to pack the buckets for the return journey.

"Those look mighty handy," the woman admitted. She fixed her eyes on Anthea again. "And you say these horses aren't sick?"

"No, ma'am," Anthea said. "And they never have been. I swear to you."

"And the king knows about this?"

"Yes, ma'am," Anthea said. "King Gareth gave the order for us to return to the north, but many of our men and horses are still in Travertine and Bellair, taking messages between the king and Queen Josephine."

Anthea didn't feel the need to mention how these messages were passed. She figured this woman had had enough revelations for one day.

"And the queen gave you that rose?" The woman pointed to Anthea's lapel.

Yes, came from Jilly via Caesar.

"No," Anthea said. She was a terrible liar, and this woman appreciated—and deserved—honesty. "My aunt Deirdre, a Rose Matron, gave it to me. I . . . attended a Rose Academy for many years."

"Interesting," the woman said. She flapped her apron, thinking. "And you say you won't need to let the horses drink from my bucket?"

"No, ma'am."

"Hmmmm."

She kept flapping, but Anthea felt her hopes surge. She could tell that the woman was going to give in. The question now was how long she would make them stand, thirsty, while she finished deciding.

Only another minute, to Anthea's relief.

"Very well," the woman said. "But use your own buckets and hurry—my man will be back for supper in an hour!"

They hurried. A bucket line formed while half the men got the horses tied up in two rows. There wasn't a bucket for every horse, so they let the horses who had been carrying riders drink first, and then led them to the end of the row while they watered the others.

But horses take a long time to drink. And they drink a lot of water. The riders were just finally topping off their own canteens when a man came down the road, leading an ox in harness.

"Uh-oh," Keth said, and punctuated this comment with a cough.

The farmer dropped the ox's lead so that it stopped a few paces away from the horses. He folded his arms over his chest and frowned at them. Anthea braced herself. Then his eyes lit on Jilly and he began to shake his head.

"Well, Miss Jillian! What have you done this time?"

"Farmer Finbar!" she crowed with delight. "Abandoned your tractor for good?"

"Oh, you girl!" He reached out and pumped her hand as though she'd been a man. "Poor machine never ran right after you and your—" He caught sight of Anthea. "Well, there you are, miss! Found your lost horses, did you?" He took in the two dozen horses crowded into his farmyard. "Looks as though you did!"

"What—" Anthea began. "Who . . . ?"

And then she remembered: the tractor coming out from behind a hedge, frightening the horses. Leonidas had spooked and gone off into the fields, dragging two mares with him. Anthea had pursued them, while Jilly and the farmer had taken care of Caesar, who had been injured, and then Jilly had gone on to Bell Hyde and the queen.

This was the same farmer.

He grabbed Anthea's hand and pumped it up and down as well. Rogers came forward, looking bemused, and offered his hand to the man.

"I'm Courier First Class Rogers," he said by way of introduction. "I hope that it's all right, but we've been drawing water from your well for the horses. And the men. We've just finished."

"Finbar, Edmund Finbar," the man said. "And you're right welcome! Of course you are!"

"Edmund!"

The riders all parted, leaving a clear path between the horses to where the farmwife stood with her hands on her hips, staring at her husband. The farmer gave Rogers an uneasy smile.

"Are you telling me that the new tractor was lost because of a *horse*?" She looked incredulous, and then uneasy, glancing at the horse nearest her as though it was waiting to smash her to the ground as well.

"Now, Jenny," he said. "I didn't want to send you into a

panic. I know how your brothers always talk about the people north of the Wall."

"You said that our tractor got out of control and ran itself into a wall." Jenny was not to be put off.

"That is true," Jilly offered. "The tractor scared the horses, Mr. Finbar jumped off to help us, and the tractor . . . kept going."

"Into a wall," Anthea said.

She had only the vaguest memories of this, but she did remember the crunching sound of metal on stone. It felt like something that had happened years ago, but it had only been six months, she realized. Hours after the tractor accident she had been shot, chased by hunters, and run right into her mother, who had put her on a private train in an attempt to win Anthea over to her mother's cause.

Jenny just stood there shaking her head. Then she started laughing.

"So you were trying to protect me from being scared by the horses?" she finally said.

"Er, yes," her husband confessed.

"Well, I just told these poor folks to hurry up and get the water before you got back, because I was trying to protect *you*," she admitted, with another chortle.

Finbar began to laugh as well, and while he was shaking hands all around, his wife went into the house and brought out pitchers of cider and cups and gave everyone a drink. She slipped some cookies into the pockets of Jilly and Anthea and Keth, and even dared to touch Buttercup's shoulder. Her husband regaled the riders with the story of how he had taken Jilly to one of the barns and hidden her and her horses there while he fetched the local animal surgeon, who had been sworn to secrecy after sewing up the gash on Caesar's shoulder.

Everyone was smiling, and Anthea felt some of the never-ending tension in her shoulders unknot, just a little. Here were more people, ordinary people, mingling with the brigade, and it was all right. They hadn't been run off the property with pitchforks. Or shot at. Slowly but surely, Anthea thought, they could get Coronam to accept the horses once again. Slowly but surely.

"Where is the surgeon?" Jilly asked as they were remounting. "If we pass by his house, I would love to thank him again!"

The laughter and smiles stopped. Anthea watched it happen, watched it fade from the faces of Jenny and Finbar, watched it spread to the riders as they noticed. The knot of tension between her shoulders tightened again.

"Oh, miss," Finbar said. "Trewes is a good man, but don't you be going anywhere near him."

"What? Why?" Jilly looked up from tying Buttercup's lead to her saddle. "He seemed all right . . . he liked the horses, didn't he?"

"That he did, miss," Finbar said. "He mentioned you again when he came last month to look at Furze." Furze was the ox. "And to tell me goodbye."

"Goodbye?"

"Aye, miss," Finbar said. He reached out and put a hand on Florian's neck. He was standing between Florian and Caesar. Florian held very still, and the farmer gingerly stroked his black mane. "His brother were a surgeon, too, down in Dawsebury, near Travertine. Seems that there's a powerful lot of sickness down that way. Coughs, fevers, and the like. His brother was taken suddenly, and so were many in the town. Trewes went for the funeral, and to get his brother's family sorted."

"And?" Jilly's voice went shrill.

"Word came two days ago," Jenny said. "All dead. The widow and the babies, Trewes, and half the town."

In the ensuing silence, Keth's cough was loud and jagged.

6

At Home at Last Farm

"HOW CAN YOU WEAR that coat all the time? It's a thousand degrees in here," Jilly said.

Anthea ignored her. It wasn't a thousand degrees in the stable. It wasn't even particularly hot. But it was warm: all the straw insulating the floors and the large animals raised the temperature significantly, but Anthea still wore her long army coat.

There was a little trickle of sweat running down her back under the coat, it was true. But what was also true was that, if she took the coat off, she felt vulnerable. The coat soothed her, like getting under a heavy blanket on a cold night. When she took it off she felt . . . light, but not in a good way. As though any breath of wind could blow her over, or that anything could cut or bruise her.

There was no one at Last Farm who would hurt her, she

knew. And she had Florian to protect her, not to mention the other horses, and Jilly and Keth, the household staff, even her fierce little owl, Arthur. But she couldn't shake the feeling that something was coming, something big and dark and terrible was about to roll over them, and she didn't want to be unprepared when it came.

In her typically uncannily shrewd fashion, Jilly said, "Keeping warm won't prevent you from getting the Dag."

Anthea shuddered. "I know," she said. "I just . . . feel like wearing my coat. I like this coat."

"We're going to be fine," Jilly told her.

"I know," Anthea said.

They were both lying, and they knew it. Over the past few days that they had been back beyond Kalabar's Wall, at Last Farm where Anthea's father and Uncle Andrew had sheltered and trained horses since before Jilly and Anthea were born, a great deal had happened in the south, and none of it was "fine."

There had been an outbreak of a terrible form of the influenza that had quickly been christened "the Dag" because the cough felt like daggers tearing through your chest. The brigade had all been terrified that Keth had it, since he still could not shake the wracking cough he had developed when he was stationed near Travertine, which is where the sickness had started.

But Keth never had a fever or any of the more debilitating symptoms of the Dag: he just couldn't stop coughing.

Dr. Hewett had mixed honey cough syrup and even boiled up some lozenges that Jilly and Anthea both kept stealing, because they were so delicious, but the doctor couldn't seem to cure his cough permanently.

Even more worrying were the continued rumors of war. No one seemed to understand what had happened that day on the river. No one seemed to want to take responsibility for it. Kronenhof swore that they had not sent those ships, and the Crown swore that they had not given the order to fire on the Kronenhofer ships, and certainly had not given the river guards the authority to completely destroy any ship. These answers, which Anthea pictured in her head as rooms full of men just shrugging and looking confused, were unsatisfactory to everyone.

Kronenhof was refusing to accept Coronam's apology, and Coronam, it must be said, wasn't actually apologizing. Anthea had pointed out that saying "I didn't do it" wasn't apologizing, and a few days later the newspaper pointed out nearly the same thing. Kronenhof had recalled their ambassador from Coronam. Coronam had taken theirs back from Kronenhof. Now other countries were involved, saying that they were going to remove their ambassadors and cut off trade, if Coronam and Kronenhof didn't apologize to each other.

Anthea knew King Gareth; he would never apologize. Orders had come from Travertine that the brigade should learn to shoot and ride "defensively." Andrew had sent his own orders, instructing them not to tell the Crown that they already knew how to shoot and that the horses were trained to fight as well. What else he had heard and seen from his new post in Travertine, Andrew didn't say.

"You see, fine," Jilly said when they left the stable.

There was a rider coming up the long drive. When some of the men in the paddocks along the drive saw him, they waved and whistled.

"Is that . . . ?" Anthea began.

The Soon King, the horses in the paddocks began to say. *The Soon King! He returns!* They whinnied greetings as Finn rode up to the yard between the big house and the stable.

From inside the stable, Florian and the others who had been put in their stalls for the night began to stamp and call out as well. Anthea and Jilly assured them that it really was Finn, which became unnecessary because as soon as Finn had dismounted, in his private paddock Constantine the herd stallion reared onto his hind legs and let out his ear-splitting scream.

Anthea hated that scream. She had first heard it the night she had come to the farm last year, and it had terrified her then. It still sent a shiver through her, reminding her of the time that she had gone into Con's paddock "uninvited" to prevent him from trampling a little owl that had wandered under the fence. Anthea had gotten the owl and herself out safely, largely thanks to Finn also jumping in to pull her out of harm's way, but Florian had been badly hurt coming to her rescue. She had been so caught up in the horror of watching Florian allow his herd stallion to bite and kick him that she had not even noticed the owl—Arthur, though he hadn't been named yet—biting hard into her hand. She had a scar from the incident.

So did Florian.

Constantine screamed again, and Anthea shuddered. Behind her, she heard Florian and Leonidas calling out, greeting Finn loudly now that the herd stallion had already done so. Marius and Caesar bugled, too, and Gaius Julius, and the other stallions that were in the stable.

But not the mares. Anthea still didn't understand the mares, and apparently neither did the stallions. Florian had once told her that the mares had other names, given to them by their mothers, shared only among themselves or with a mate, and sometimes not even then. Florian had also told her that it was "not his place" to directly address a mare, and even though he and Bluebell got along very well (as far as Anthea could tell) they would often speak through her even when they were walking side by side, like young schoolchildren having a fight.

Finn tied Marius's reins behind his neck so they wouldn't get tangled and sent him into his paddock with his bridle and saddle still on. He threw his saddlebags over his shoulder and came toward Anthea and Jilly, who were hurrying over to meet him. He grinned when he saw them and held out his free arm.

Anthea stopped short, but Jilly went ahead and gave him a hug.

"You're finally back from your mysterious mission!" Jilly said.

Finn made a face. "Just more nonsense messages. Honestly, at first I think Gareth just wanted to give me extra work."

He turned to Anthea, hesitated at her stiff expression, and then patted her awkwardly on the shoulder. He had kissed her once, on the cheek, and they had never spoken of it or repeated it. Anthea wondered if he remembered. She certainly did.

"Where's Dr. Hewett?" Finn said. "I need to speak to him immediately."

"Oh, in his cottage, I think," Anthea said. "Why? Are you sick?"

She and Jilly both took a step backward. Anthea couldn't even feel embarrassed: the Dag sounded horrible.

"No, no, I'm fine," Finn assured them. "But I've got a bunch of people with me, and they need lodgings and a place to work."

"What?" Anthea looked around. "Where?"

"Back at the station," Finn explained. "Scientists studying the Dag."

Jilly put her hands on her hips. "What did you bring them here for?"

"It wasn't my idea!" Finn held up his hands in self-defense. "The king ordered me to lead them here!"

"You could have at least sent a warning ahead," Jilly grumbled.

Finn sighed. "Con does *not* like this idea. He doesn't want any strangers near the herd. He flat-out refused to pass along the message."

Anthea shot a look at Constantine, and found to her discomfort that he was watching her already. She looked quickly away but could feel that the herd stallion did not. She turned her back on him and covered her unease by peering down the lane in the deepening twilight, even though she couldn't see the Wall, let alone the train station.

"We need to get out the motorcar to fetch them," Finn said. "That's why I'm looking for Dr. Hewett. He knows how to drive."

"So do I," Anthea said.

Although she had no memories of the last time she had driven. She knew she had done something with a motorcar on a moving train, but there was a large blank spot after that, and Florian refused to talk about it. It was far too terrifying, he claimed.

Still, her former headmistress, Miss Miniver, had insisted that all the girls learn to drive, and Anthea was sure she could remember the basics. Certainly well enough to drive down the lane and out to the train station to fetch a few doctors.

"If you're sure," Finn said doubtfully.

"You can drive?" Jilly sounded jealous. "You've never driven *me* anywhere!"

"We have *horses*," Anthea pointed out. "And no motorcar."

"Right, true," Jilly agreed easily. "Finn, you want to go find Dr. Hewett? I'll show Anthea the Thing."

"What thing?" Anthea asked nervously.

"You know, Papa's motorcar. The Thing."

"That . . . that *thing* Caillin MacRennie fetched me from the station with?"

Anthea stopped dead as Jilly led her toward a shed that she had never noticed before, tucked between the big house and the cottage where Nurse Shannon and Keth lived. Anthea remembered that motorcar, if it could even be called such. It looked like an old oxcart someone had strapped an engine to.

"Yes, that's why we call it the Thing," Jilly said.

She grabbed one of the doors of the shed without waiting for Anthea to follow and hauled it open. In the dimness within Anthea could barely make out the awkward bulk of the Thing. Maybe she should wait for Dr. Hewett.

While she hesitated, Jilly grabbed the back of the Thing and tried to drag it out of the shed. Anthea heard a grinding sound and saw the way the wheels were locked and ran to stop her cousin.

"Stop! There's a brake on," she said. "Just . . . I'll do it."

"Can I come?"

"Will there be room for us all? How many scientists did he bring? And will they have luggage?" Anthea looked doubtfully at the two rough bench seats and the little luggage space at the back.

"Oh, fine." Jilly pouted as Anthea tried to find the brake release. "I'll saddle up Caesar and—"

"Could you please get some rooms ready?" Anthea said.

She released the brake and Jilly had to jump back as the Thing rolled backward and nearly went right over her foot. "Find out from Finn how many we need and just . . . play hostess, all right?"

"Fine," Jilly agreed, but she stayed to watch Anthea try and figure out the controls of the Thing.

Anthea was convinced, after about five minutes, that neither Uncle Andrew nor Caillin MacRennie had ever seen an actual motorcar. Everything was sort of, but not really, in the right place, and they were sort of, but not really, the right shape and size.

The Thing didn't purr like her uncle Daniel's elegant new motorcar: it coughed and spluttered and gasped. Jilly moved even farther away, which Anthea thought very wise. She cranked the steering wheel, which was not a circle but shaped like the number eight lying on its side, and managed to get the Thing pointed toward the lane without smashing into the wall of the shed, which she thought rather a triumph.

Finn and Dr. Hewett came out of the big house just then, but Anthea had the motorcar going and feared—from the noises that it made—that if it stopped it would not start up again. She waved with what she hoped was a casual air as she passed them and then turned her attention to keeping the Thing headed down the drive. It had the tendency to veer to the right, and she didn't want to crash into the fence.

As she made her loud, slow way to the Wall, Anthea thought how much easier it would have been on horseback. Of course, none of the scientists could ride, and if they brought large trunks they would be impossible to tie onto a horse's back. She began daydreaming about ways that she could hitch an oxcart to a team of horses, using straps attached to their saddles instead of a heavy ox collar.

Beloved? It was Florian, suddenly, in her thoughts. *Where are you going? What is that thing?*

Oh, no. She was almost to the Wall and Florian . . . she hadn't told Florian what she was doing. He had probably smelled the grease and dust of the Thing as she went by the stable, and sensed her presence moving away from him.

I have to take this motorcar to the train station, she sent back. *I have to pick up some men who cannot ride.*

Motorcar? Florian's mind filled with panic. *Her motorcar?*

Anthea realized that the only motorcar that Florian knew was her mother's. Even if her memories of it were few, his were not. He hadn't been sick; he had been the one who had gotten her safely away from her mother.

No, no, she assured him as she slowed down within sight of the gates of Kalabar's Wall. *It's Uncle Andrew's motorcar! Caillin MacRennie used it to bring me to the farm. To you, my love! Do you remember? I will be right back. Jilly is home, and Finn.*

She had thought this would be reassuring. She was wrong.

You are alone?

Don't you dare try to break out of the stable and follow me! she replied swiftly.

She had finally brought the car to a creaking, coughing

halt at the gate, and she was sure that the guard would think she was daft. She had her face screwed up and was holding up a finger for silence to make sure that she sent the right combination of words and tone to Florian. The last thing she wanted was for him to injure himself trying to bash down the door of his stall and come to her, and she told him so.

I will be back tonight, she said firmly. *And you will wait there for me. I am sure that Finn and Marius are coming to help me. Finn did not take off Marius's tack. I am sure they are riding out again.*

A tangle of worry was still coming from Florian, but the Wall guards were now staring at her. She had a hard time talking to Florian and humans at the same time, so she just sent her horse a reassuring pulse of love and smiled charmingly at the guards.

The chief guard recognized her, but his eyes went immediately back to the Thing. He looked far more shocked to see her driving a motorcar than riding a horse, and came over to the side of the vehicle with a worried frown.

"Miss Thornley, is something wrong at the farm?"

"No, no, it's just that I have to fetch some people from the train station," she assured him.

"You alone, miss?"

He was just as bad as Florian, Anthea thought. And so she used the same technique on him. "I am indeed alone," she said. "But I know how to drive, and I am quite capable."

"My next question," the guard said, "is are you sure this thing is safe? For anyone?"

"That's a grand deal o' smoke," the other guard observed. "I've ne'er seen a mo'orcar smoke so much." He hesitated. "Even this one."

"Oh, it's fine, it's fine," Anthea said. "May I?"

"Well, all right, but you be careful," the guard sergeant said.

He and his fellow guard undid the bar and slid back the heavy iron gates that guarded the four-foot-thick gray stone wall. Anthea managed to get the car into gear again and moving, but it was a near thing. She wondered if she should drive slowly past the train station and tell their guests to just jump on. The sergeant was still shaking his head in worry as she passed.

"He's worse than Florian," she muttered to herself.

Although it was certainly a nice change from the way they had come and gone through the Wall before the king had acknowledged them. It used to be that you had to use papers to get through, and there was a check of your luggage, and they didn't dare bring the horses through at all. The guards had suspected that the animals at the Last Farm were . . . unusual, but had turned a blind eye to it. Anthea suspected that her uncle had bribed them. She had been confused, too, when she had first arrived last year that she hadn't needed some sort of documentation to travel past the Wall, but it had turned out that that was because she had been born in the north. The next time she had passed through that gate, on a mission, going from the north to the south, she had to show her Leanan birth certificate and state her business for the official record.

But then, the last time she and Jilly had gone through, with several of the other riders, they had gotten a friendly wave from that same sergeant, and nothing more. Things were certainly very different now.

She made it to the train station without the Thing stopping or exploding. It was past sunset, but the lamps around the station were lit and she could clearly see a group of adults standing around the edge of the platform with a large group of trunks. She would have to make several trips, or they would have to see if the station master could hire them an oxcart this late in the day.

"About time," someone said as she pulled up next to the platform and slipped on the brake without turning off the engine.

"At least they've sent a woman this time," another voice said.

Anthea looked up at the group gathered on the platform and saw that they were all women. She blinked rapidly. Women *scientists*? Were they real? She barely kept herself from saying it aloud.

"Well, a girl," the scientist said when she got a good look at Anthea. "But at least it's a start."

7

SCIENTISTS IN THE BARN

ALL THE SCIENTISTS WERE indeed women. They claimed they had been sent by "the Crown," but in the little time that Anthea had spent with them, she heard them all mention Queen Josephine several times, but never the king. It didn't surprise her at all. Though she had grown up thinking that the queen and her Rose Maidens' activities mainly included tea parties and poetry readings, Anthea had since learned that the queen had a lot of quite varied interests and that her Rose Maidens' skills ranged from being exceptional at styling hair to being versed in Coronami law to spying on the king's ministers.

Although that last was largely speculation on Jilly's part. The queen had hinted about such things, but never said it outright.

Jilly, however, was quick to point out that Anthea's mother

had been a Rose Maiden, and now she was definitely a spy. Which Anthea could hardly deny.

The Crown, in whatever form, had charged the lady scientists to find a cure for the Dag. They were from the queen's newly founded Science Academy for Women. Some of them had trained as nurses before the academy opened, and now they were going back to study more of the things they were passionate about, like the workings of the brain or the spreading of diseases.

"Diseases?" Jilly asked in disbelief as she helped unpack one of the crates. She looked at the titles of the books she was putting up on a makeshift bookcase made of planks and bricks. "You like to read about diseases?"

Anthea honestly thought that the woman, who was called Dr. Rosemary and who was the group's leader, was going to smack Jilly. Anthea hurried to intervene, taking the last book out of Jilly's hand and putting it on the shelf with great care.

"What else do you need?" she asked quickly.

"Plenty of light, water, and *quiet*," Dr. Rosemary told her.

"We can do that," Anthea said. "Anything else?"

She still could not understand why the women had been sent all the way beyond the Wall to do their research. Surely the building where they usually worked was better equipped than this barn? And there had been no letter of explanation for Uncle Andrew, nothing but what Finn had said about being told to escort them north, and what Dr. Rosemary said about being told to come here by the Crown.

Dr. Rosemary looked at Anthea, and Anthea wished for the hundredth time that the Way allowed her to understand what *people* were thinking. The woman's face was absolutely blank, and although Anthea was sure that Dr. Rosemary didn't like her, she told herself that that was impossible. The woman had just met her, and Anthea had tried her best to be helpful. Why would she hate Anthea? When Anthea had picked them up at the train station, they had all seemed pleased to see a young woman driving and giving orders. But just moments later, Dr. Rosemary had gone stiff and stopped speaking to Anthea unless absolutely necessary.

"Light, water, and quiet," Dr. Rosemary repeated, her tone repressive.

"You won't be bringing any patients here, though?" Dr. Hewett asked from the doorway. He came limping into the barn. "We aren't really equipped for more than a handful, unless you want to move your laboratory into the big house?"

"We don't need patients," Dr. Rosemary said. "We went to a hospital in the capital before we left and took plenty of samples."

She nodded toward another scientist who was carefully unpacking glass jars and tubes from a wooden chest full of straw padding. The other scientist looked over, questioning, then went back to carefully setting out her equipment.

Anthea took an involuntary step back. Samples? Samples of the sickness that was killing so many people? She saw that

Dr. Rosemary was watching her and put her chin up, but she didn't step forward and she kept her hands behind her back.

"They're perfectly safe as long as no one tampers with them," Dr. Rosemary said, and she looked pointedly at Anthea as though tampering with her samples was something Anthea had been caught doing before.

"What are they?" Anthea asked, choosing to ignore the accusatory look.

She was still repulsed, but a sort of fascination had sunk in. How did one take samples of a cough?

"We have blood and saliva as well as sputum from several patients, male and female, and different ages," Dr. Rosemary said.

"Sputum?" Anthea asked, against her better judgment.

"Ew," Jilly said, putting out a hand to stop the scientist.

"Matter coughed up from the lungs of the sick person," Dr. Rosemary said, arching an eyebrow at Jilly.

Anthea felt her skin crawl. She wanted to take another step away from the samples but felt like Dr. Rosemary was challenging her. The woman had been challenging her since Anthea had met her at the train station, and Anthea didn't particularly care for it. Nor did she understand the reason behind it. Dr. Rosemary seemed to take it as a personal affront that there were only two female riders in the Horse Brigade, and that they were so young besides, but that was hardly Anthea's fault.

Anthea had perhaps spent three hours in Dr. Rosemary's

presence that day, and she was already coming to dislike her, which made her feel rather sad. A woman scientist! Why did she have to be so . . . impolite? Dr. Rosemary had turned up her nose at sweet Miss Ravel's offer of help, since she was merely a Rose Academy trained schoolteacher and not "a real scientist." She refused to speak to Finn, preferring to direct all her remarks to Dr. Hewett, and all her demands to Anthea and Jilly, though she didn't seem to care for them any more than she cared for Miss Ravel.

The girls had tried to excuse themselves from unpacking by saying that they had lessons, but Dr. Rosemary had informed them that they would learn more helping her. Anthea hardly thought that stacking books on shelves and trying not to touch anything that might be infected with a sick person's spit was the same as their very well-regulated school lessons. But she didn't argue.

Jilly nudged Anthea and then cleared her throat. Anthea excused them by pointing out that it was time for them to take care of their horses. Dr. Rosemary looked sour at this, but Dr. Hewett waved them away with a smile.

The girls hurried away before Dr. Rosemary could find something else for them to do. As soon as they were out of earshot, Jilly started to ask the questions she hadn't been able to before.

"Have you talked to Finn? Did he tell you?"

"Tell me about what? I've been with you the whole time,"

Anthea said. "Except when I was driving to and from the train station."

"Well, I managed to corner Finn this morning after breakfast," Jilly said. "And it's bad."

"What is?"

Anthea stopped, and then noticed that Arthur was stalking across the gravel in front of the big house toward them. She crouched down and held out her hands, and the little owl walked into them. She straightened and tucked him into her jacket, where he settled down to sleep at once. The housekeeper and her girls were scrambling to get all the spare rooms aired out and Anthea reckoned that they must have cleaned her room a little too vigorously and woken up the owl.

"The *Dag*, Thea," Jilly said. "The Dag is very, very bad." She took a deep breath. "A lot of people are dying."

"How many?" Anthea's voice was suddenly hoarse.

"They . . . they don't even know. It's spreading so rapidly, and it's so hard to keep track now. There's been over a hundred, though. I mean, there had been when the queen asked Finn to bring her scientists here. So I would guess there's been a lot more."

"So it really was the queen? And not the king?" Anthea grimaced as they stepped into the dimness of the stable. "All these years of revering the Crown," she muttered. "It's not the Crown, it's—"

Jilly stopped her outside of Bluebell's stall with a hand on her arm.

"Now, you know that I don't have any particularly fond feelings toward the king, or the Crown," she said. "So when I say I think he's trying, you know it means something."

"You think he's trying?" Anthea unlatched Bluebell's stall and set Arthur on the mare's hanging net of hay. "Trying to do what, though?"

"He's . . . well. According to Finn," Jilly said. "He's . . ."

"He hasn't denounced us yet," Finn said grimly, coming out of another stall, leading Marius. "Despite the fact that everyone blames the horses for the Dag."

Beloved, are you all right? Florian stuck his head over the door of his stall, anxious at the burst of emotion that had just come from her.

They speak of death, Bluebell told him. *Is this war?*

The smells from the foals' barn are worrisome, Leonidas said. *It smells like the place where Domitian is herd stallion now.*

Anthea wasn't sure what he meant. Unless he wasn't used to so many women being around. But he had never had a problem with it before.

Other horse heads protruded over other stall doors, though fortunately many of the horses were still in the south with their riders, and a few more were out in the paddocks. Still, there were a dozen or so now kicking anxiously at their doors and laying their ears back.

"What did you do?"

Two riders came hurrying into the stable, still pulling on

their jackets. They had apparently been having a very leisurely morning—with Uncle Andrew still in the south, there was a general holiday air around the farm. But when they saw Finn they both straightened and saluted before going at once to their horses.

"Who's died?" the first man asked after stroking his stallion's nose.

"Oh, charming," said the other. "I didn't want him to know about the Dag," he whispered loudly.

Finn rolled his shoulders back and twisted his neck from side to side.

"All right," he said at last, addressing the girls and the men. "You may as well all know. Andrew wanted me to make a formal announcement, but I hate that kind of thing. So just feel free to tell whomever you need to, send them to me if they want to ask questions.

"I guess."

They waited. Anthea felt a heaviness in her mind, and she wondered if Constantine was eavesdropping on Finn as well.

"A lot of people are dying—have died—from the Dag," he said at last. "And by a lot, I mean over two hundred that we know of, and that number is almost a week old now. Many, many more are sick, and will die if we don't find a cure. Hospitals are full, and people are panicking.

"Panicking, and blaming horses."

"Isn't that just like the southerners," one of the men said, and spat into the straw.

Anthea arched one eyebrow at him. She had, after all, spent most of her life to date in the south. And also, that spit had come awfully close to her boots. The man looked abashed, but didn't apologize.

"Look at it from their point of view," Finn said. "They've been told for generations that horses bring disease, and within weeks of horses being allowed south of the Wall again, a mysterious illness spreads across the country."

Anthea opened her mouth, and closed it again. She felt her eyes going wide. Jilly suddenly slapped her on the shoulder.

"Ow! What is wrong with you?" Anthea demanded, rubbing the sore spot Jilly's blow left.

"I could see you thinking it," Jilly said. "I know how your little Rose Maiden brain works."

"I thought you liked the Rose Maidens now," Anthea said stiffly, to cover the fact that just for one fleeting second she had indeed worried that horses were causing the Dag.

"I like the queen, so I am all right with *her* Rose Maidens," Jilly said. "And the princesses. And occasionally wearing a rose myself."

"Anthea's suspicion is the reason why the scientists are here," Finn said loudly. "The first reported cases of the Dag, and the first deaths, all happened in three places: Bellaire, the Crownlands, and West Coro."

Jilly gasped and her hands flew to her mouth. Anthea realized that she was rubbing Bluebell's nose so hard she was in danger of hurting the poor mare, and forced herself to stop.

But Bluebell butted her head against Anthea's shoulder and Anthea grabbed her mane for comfort.

Bellaire. The Crownlands. West Coro.

The three places where there were Horse Brigade outposts. Other places, mostly military bases, had a single horse and rider so that they could relay messages. The foggy, awful posting where Caillin MacRennie was, and where Anthea and Jilly had been until last week, was West Coro. Finn had been at Bellaire, which was near the queen's residence at Bell Hyde. And Andrew went back and forth between West Coro and the Crownlands, a bucolic suburb of Travertine where many of the wealthy had summer homes.

Like Anthea's uncle Daniel and aunt Deirdre.

"If you're going to send word to your aunt and uncle," Finn said, swiftly reading Anthea's expression, as he did so often, "do it now. There's a rumor they'll start quarantining the more heavily affected areas, to prevent the disease spreading."

"If Uncle Andrew is still there," Anthea began, but Finn was already shaking his head.

"They're coming home. All of them. Until people stop panicking," Finn said.

"Won't that make people think there's something to hide?" Jilly asked.

"What if they are sick and it spreads?" Anthea asked at the same time.

"Anthea!" Jilly smacked her again.

"But it's a real problem, Miss Jilly," one of the other riders said. "Just because it's not the horses that caused the Dag, doesn't mean we can't get it, too."

"I know it's not the horses that caused the Dag," Anthea said loudly, glaring at Jilly and thinking of giving her a smack on the shoulder just because. "But I don't want it to spread if some riders are already sick. And I really want to know what *did* cause it, and how it started in those three places at the same time."

"Don't we all," Finn said.

8

THE QUARANTINE

LEISURELY RIDES ALONG THE Leanan coast stopped. Mornings having a cozy lie-in followed by a stroll to the stable, then school lessons followed by a long lunch stopped as well. The dinner gong, once the signal that it was time for a delicious family meal with Uncle Andrew and Jilly and Caillin Mac-Rennie and their friends, now became the constant reminder that something was terribly wrong.

They had come back to Leana: the riders, the horses, all of them. It should have been wonderful, after weeks and even months apart, carrying coded messages between army stations. Especially since they had never been told what the messages meant, or whom they were intended for. There were rumors that it was all a big test of the brigade's loyalty, and that the messages were meaningless. The horses and riders were anxious to be back at the farm, among friends.

But a third of the riders had symptoms of the Dag when they arrived, and more succumbed every day. The big barn had been divided in half lengthwise, and one side was a long hospital ward, while the other was the laboratory. When that was too full, the small cottages where the men lived were turned into hospital wards as well, and even the men who were still strong enough to get around were ordered to stay inside.

Which meant that there were a great many horses to care for. Everyone who wasn't sick had to take turns feeding, mucking, grooming, and exercising the horses. Even Miss Ravel, who didn't have the Way like her brother, and usually only indulged in a trot around the paddocks on a dainty chestnut mare named Daffodil, could be found pushing a wheelbarrow full of fouled straw out to the dung heap in the morning.

She would call out math problems and they would yell back the answer, or she might throw out the name of a country and they would have to name the capital city and principal exports. Even the adult riders got into this and liked to try beating the students in calling out the correct answer first. Miss Ravel had assigned reading, a heavily symbolic Kronenhofer novel translated into Coronami, and Anthea was entertained to find that several of the riders were reading it, too, and voicing strong opinions about the terrible life choices that Werther, the main character, was making.

The raucous group lessons were the most entertaining part of what was happening at Last Farm. And nothing else was even remotely close to entertaining.

Anthea didn't mind the work, though. She didn't even mind exercising a variety of horses, which Finn pointed out had improved her riding considerably, since Florian and even Bluebell let her get away with a sloppy seat and slack reins. (She had, of course, thrown a wet sponge at him for that remark.) But she greatly minded the reason for it.

There were fifty-three riders, ranging in age from Caillin MacRennie (who refused to comment anything other than that he was older than motorcars) to Keth, who was a year younger than Anthea and Jilly. They could also count Miss Ravel among the riders, unofficially, and Keth's mother, Nurse Shannon, could be persuaded onto the oldest and most sedate mares when necessary. Which meant a grand total of fifty-five people who could back a horse.

Thirty-two of them were sick. And that included Uncle Andrew.

The sick were kept separate from the healthy, except for Dr. Hewett and the scientists, who wore masks and long hospital gowns over their clothes and had the maids boil them clean along with the sheets and towels used by their patients. Uncle Andrew was still well enough to pass orders through Dr. Hewett, though many of the other patients were not. Those who were too weak to sit up or even feed themselves were kept in the barn so that the scientists could help the doctor and Nurse Shannon take care of them.

Anthea also suspected that it was so Dr. Rosemary and the

other scientists could study them. They had their samples, true, but despite Dr. Rosemary's comments about Rose Academies, Anthea had studied science under a stern science teacher in Travertine, and she knew that it was always better to study live subjects. Anthea knew that they needed to find a cure, but she wasn't sure how she felt about her uncle and others among the riders being the live test subjects.

As though summoned by her thoughts, she saw Dr. Rosemary approaching the paddock where Anthea was exercising the mares. She did this by riding Bluebell, and shouting at the other mares to get them to run around, with Bluebell chasing them.

If Arthur could be bothered to stay awake, he would help by swooping over their heads and hooting, but if the sun was too bright he tended to bite and try to hide instead. Anthea had gotten used to leaving the window of her bedroom open a crack so that he could come and go at night, even though it let in a draft.

So for now Anthea was charging Bluebell back and forth across the mares' big paddock and cawing like a deranged crow to make them move. She had nudged them repeatedly through the Way, but they seemed to enjoy ignoring her. Several of the mares were getting quite plump. Anthea had never paid much attention to how the riders had exercised the mares before, but surely it couldn't have been this hard.

Despite the scientist's clear dislike of Anthea, she was

more than willing to stop when Dr. Rosemary came to stand at the side of the paddock and leaned her arms on the top rail of the fence. The older woman had her blond hair back in a tight knot and Anthea could see paler threads of white at the temples. Dr. Rosemary's eyes were tired, and the long white coat she wore over her sensible gray skirt and white blouse was clean but very crumpled looking.

Anthea rode Bluebell up to the fence. Dr. Rosemary didn't flinch or move her arms, even when Bluebell nuzzled her sleeve to see if the scientist had any sugar or apples hidden there. But she did hold very still, the way someone facing a wild animal would. Anthea didn't say or do anything, and after making certain that there were no treats to be had, Bluebell dropped her dappled gray head and began to graze.

Dr. Rosemary breathed out rather loudly, and then lifted one arm off the fence to nervously smooth her hair.

"They don't bite," Anthea said.

That was a bit of a lie. *Bluebell* wasn't prone to biting, and so long as they kept Dr. Rosemary away from Leonidas or Gaius Julius, it would be true. She had been warned, as had all the scientists, not to go near Constantine or his private paddock.

"Miss Cross-Thornley," Dr. Rosemary began.

"Thornley. Just Miss Thornley," Anthea interjected. "Or Anthea. Is fine."

"Anthea, then," Dr. Rosemary said. She seemed a little

startled by Anthea's rejection of her full name. "Your uncle said the same thing," she murmured. "Anthea, I am going to need your help," she finished quickly, before Anthea could ask what her uncle had said.

"If you need a ride to the station, you will have to wait until I am finished here," Anthea said.

"I meant for my research," Dr. Rosemary said stiffly. "I'm afraid you haven't gotten rid of me so easily."

Anthea stared at the woman. Did she really think . . . ?

"I'm not trying to get rid of you," Anthea said. "What have I ever done to make you think I want you gone?"

Bluebell stirred, raising her head from the grass and pawing the ground with a hoof. Florian whinnied a question from across the field. Dr. Rosemary took a step back, looking from the mare to Anthea.

"Well, *you* haven't done anything," Dr. Rosemary began. "And, well, I shouldn't have brought it up. What is important now is that I need your help."

Anthea wanted to just ride away. Jilly or Finn could help, if they wanted to, but Anthea didn't want to be anywhere near Dr. Rosemary. Bluebell took a few quick steps away from the fence, ready to race toward her fellows at the slightest nudge.

When Anthea didn't look at her or say anything, Dr. Rosemary forged ahead.

"We need samples."

Anthea looked at her. They had samples. They were

surrounded by sick people, and had brought other samples with them.

"From the horses," Dr. Rosemary clarified.

Bluebell took another step away from the woman, and Anthea didn't blame her.

"None of the horses are sick, correct? Some of their riders have the Dag, but not the horses? I mean, you could tell if they were, could you not?"

The smell doesn't stick to us, Bluebell remarked.

Anthea stroked her mane. She didn't know what Bluebell meant, but she knew none of the horses liked the scientists because of the odors of chemicals on their clothes.

Of course not, darling, you smell of wind and hay, Anthea assured her.

"No, none of the horses are sick," Anthea said aloud.

"I suspected before I came, and I still believe, that the horses have some sort of immunity that we could use to formulate a cure," Dr. Rosemary said.

"Yes," Anthea said. "Although my understanding is that humans and animals don't get the same illnesses very often. So I don't know that horses are really the key."

"True," Dr. Rosemary said, looking startled and a little pleased.

"Miss Ravel is really an excellent teacher," Anthea remarked, doing her best not to snap.

"Er, yes," Dr. Rosemary admitted. "But because of this

strong bond . . . this Way . . . which makes them slightly more than an ox or a dog . . . I suspect that we have more in common with them and so there might be shared elements that we could exploit."

"Exploit?"

"Use," Dr. Rosemary said, though the word wasn't much better. "We need samples from the horses . . . which I haven't mentioned before because I initially thought that we would be able to simply take them," she continued.

Anthea's attention had gone to the stallions, who still hovered by the fence and were steadily growing distressed. She wasn't sure if they were eavesdropping on Dr. Rosemary, and she was trying to reassure them, but now her head whipped around, her hair stringing across her face.

"*Take* samples? You mean blood and saliva? From *my* horses? Without *my* permission?"

Dr. Rosemary closed her eyes. "We thought it would be easier. We didn't think they would be so big and . . . intelligent."

"You thought you would be taking samples from dogs, not dragons," Anthea said coolly.

"Precisely." Dr. Rosemary plucked at the cuff of her long coat. "Will you . . . help us . . . collect samples from the horses? We want to compare them to the samples we have of those who are not sick, so we can see the similarities."

"Do none of you have the Way?" Anthea asked. "Jilly is

dying to ask. And since you're actually speaking to me right now, I might as well."

Dr. Rosemary looked horrified at the very idea. "Certainly not!"

Anthea could tell that Dr. Rosemary was telling the truth. But she wondered if the rest of the scientists should be asked, in private.

No, Bluebell said.

Pardon?

None of them have the Way, Bluebell told her. *We tried when they first came. They cannot hear us. We mares were enthralled at the idea of so many women in one place. Our place. But they cannot hear us.*

That is a shame, Anthea said.

Bluebell flicked her tail and nickered in agreement. Dr. Rosemary gave a little jump. Some of the scientists had expressed an interest in the horses, beyond wanting to study them, but none of them had taken to it the way the queen and princesses had. Anthea heaved a little sigh. It would have made things so much easier!

"So you need us to help you collect saliva, which is easy enough, and blood, not so much?" Anthea said.

"Yes, and—"

"Getting a horse to cough isn't as easy as you think," Anthea interjected.

She noticed that Jilly was heading her way, riding Caesar

and leading two more stallions. Anthea both wanted and didn't want her cousin to be the next person to hear about the samples. Anthea looked around for Finn, and gave Marius a nudge when she couldn't see him.

Then Dr. Rosemary's words struck Anthea. None of the horses were sick. One man had coughed so hard he vomited across his stallion's mane, but his horse was just fine.

"*None* of the horses are sick," Anthea whispered.

"No, not even the ones who came from the south, near the original outbreak."

The smell doesn't stick to us, Bluebell said again.

Anthea still didn't understand what the mare meant, so she let that comment go and asked Dr. Rosemary.

"So the Dag *isn't* the illness that killed the horses and the Leanans back before the Wall was built?"

"Oh, heavens, no!" Dr. Rosemary said. "That caused oozing sores and loss of circulation in the extremities. Many of the survivors lost fingers and toes. It was very well documented. I'm sure I can find you a book on it."

Anthea shuddered and shook her head, but pressed on.

"Does the queen know? The king?"

"Of course. I have put it in my reports," Dr. Rosemary said. "But they knew that before we came here."

"Does everyone know that? Was an official announcement made?" Anthea pressed.

"I have no idea," Dr. Rosemary said. She looked at Anthea

as though seeing her for the first time. "Your loyalty is entirely to these animals, isn't it? And not . . . anyone else?"

"If you are implying that I'm a traitor to the Crown," Anthea began hotly.

But then she stopped and put her hand on Bluebell's neck. She *was* more loyal to her horses than the Crown, if the Crown meant King Gareth. And that made her want to shout from the rooftops of Travertine that the horses didn't cause the Dag.

Jilly and now Finn were headed toward them, sparing Anthea the need to finish.

"What's going on?" Finn asked with false casualness. "The horses are getting stirred up."

"We are going to help Dr. Rosemary and her colleagues take samples from the horses," Anthea said with as much confidence as she could muster. She saw Jilly's eyes widen, and her cousin's mouth opened, but Anthea kept going. "And when they find a cure for the Dag, we are going to deliver it personally, first to Travertine, and then to the rest of Coronam!"

9

LETTERS AND MAPS

ANTHEA WANTED THE HORSES to ride up, triumphant, into Travertine Palace Square with saddlebags full of a cure for the Dag, but that was not to be. At least not yet. Though they had taken samples from all the horses, and carefully marked which horses had been away from the farm and which had sick riders, science was a slow, meticulous process, as Dr. Rosemary testily informed Anthea a week later.

"But we can still help," Anthea yelled through Uncle Andrew's door.

There was some coughing, and then a shuffling and dragging sound. Crouched outside Andrew's door, Anthea sat back on her haunches, but Jilly moved closer. Finn, who had been standing over them looking disapproving, finally sat down cross-legged between the girls.

"How?" Uncle Andrew said.

He was apparently sitting just on the other side of his door. Anthea tried to edge away from the crack under the door without making it too obvious. Jilly, sensibly, did too.

"We've gotten almost no mail from the south," Anthea told him. "Not like I'm expecting much." She did her best not to sound bitter. "But I *did* send a letter to Uncle Daniel and Aunt Deirdre, asking if they were all right, and haven't gotten a response. The queen says that she has checked on them, and they are all right, or were, but that the regular mail service has been mostly suspended."

"Most deliveries have stopped," Finn said. "And the trains are running very irregularly."

"But we're not," Jilly said, eyes gleaming. "We could set up relay stations and pass things along. Mail. Eggs. Other goods."

"We're not strapping huge cans of milk to the horses," Finn said.

"Let's start with the mail," Uncle Andrew said. He coughed. "It's regulated by the Crown." Another cough, longer this time.

"Anthea and I have both written to the queen already," Jilly said.

"Sorry," Anthea immediately added.

After last year's debacle when she had nearly caused a war (or so it seemed to her) by hiding her correspondence from her uncle, she had tried to be more forthcoming about such things.

But she also didn't really like showing her letters to everyone on the farm before she got "permission" to send them.

"No, no, that's fine," Andrew said. "Has she any news of interest?"

"Lots of people are sick," Jilly supplied.

"And she doesn't write very often, which I find worrisome," Anthea put in. "She says she's not ill, but . . ."

They all sat in silence for a minute. There was some quiet coughing from the other side of the door. Then they heard footsteps coming up the stairs. Anthea assumed it was one of the maids or Caillin MacRennie, and continued to fiddle with the horseshoe charm around her neck. She had braided together some hairs from Florian's, Leonidas's, and Blue-bell's tails, as was traditional in Leana, but it was scratchy and she was starting to think that putting the charm back on the silver chain Finn had given her might be more comfortable. All of a sudden, Jilly kicked Anthea's ankle.

"Ouch! Why did you—"

It wasn't Caillin MacRennie or one of the maids who had come upstairs. It was Dr. Rosemary.

"Captain Thornley," Dr. Rosemary called through the door. "It's Dolly Rosemary."

Jilly kicked Anthea's ankle again, more subtly this time, but Anthea couldn't look at her. She knew exactly what Jilly's face would look like, and she couldn't risk offending Dr. Rosemary by cracking a smile. Anthea had assumed that Rosemary was the doctor's first name, and that calling her Dr. Rosemary was a sort of quaint familiarity on the part of her colleagues. Anthea would not for a million years have suspected that the scientist's given name was Dolly.

"Yes, Doctor?" Uncle Andrew called politely back through the door.

"I need more samples," Dr. Rosemary said. "I need to track the disease, gather it from people in different stages."

"You are welcome to collect samples from any of the riders," Uncle Andrew said. "And you've taken samples from the horses already, correct?"

"Yes, I've tested all the horses and the riders," Dr. Rosemary said. "Now I need samples from farther afield.

"I need people of different backgrounds, from different locations that were hit by the disease at different times. The farm is too homogenous to give me all the information that I need. The only way to devise a cure is to take this disease apart and see all the pieces."

She looked down at the young people huddled on the floor. She clenched her fist, but not in a threatening way.

"It's almost . . . it's like it's on the tip of my tongue," she said, mostly to them. "It's maddening."

They all nodded. Anthea wasn't even sure what she meant, and then thought of the first days at the farm, when the Way had just been heating up in her brain, and her memories of riding had still felt like dreams. It was a maddening feeling, to know something but not be able to understand it.

"All right," Uncle Andrew said, sounding more than a little baffled. "You . . . can do as you like, I can't stop you."

"I want to use the brigade," Dr. Rosemary said. "The horses will move faster than someone on foot, and can get into more places than the train. I heard the children talking about delivering mail. Could they not also bring me samples?"

In the long silence that followed, the clock in the downstairs entry hall chimed the time loudly.

"Dinner!" Jilly said brightly.

"Even through the door I know you're planning on going, Jillian," her father said. "So I may as well give my permission."

"Hooray!" Jilly said. "Real work!"

"Hooray," Anthea said flatly. "We might all get the Dag."

"You don't have to go if you don't want to," Finn said. "And I don't mean that in a threatening way," he added.

"Of course she doesn't," Uncle Andrew said. "Volunteers only, for something like this.

"Yes, Jilly, I can feel you raising your hand to volunteer!" her father said, just as Jilly did indeed raise her hand.

"Now Finn," he continued, "write a letter to the king. Tell him that we're going to send teams of horses out. Not very many, because of the sick riders, but some. Ask him where they should go, but make sure it's in line with what Dr. Rosemary wants. We can deliver letters and light packages, and take samples . . . or ask the local doctors for samples? Again, I'm sure Dr. Rosemary knows what she wants."

"Yes, sir," Finn said.

"Anthea?"

"Yes?"

"Queen Josephine," he said, and didn't need to explain.

"Naturally," she said.

Anthea had already started a letter to the queen before they had gone to talk to Andrew through the door. Now she went back to her room and sat at her desk, staring at the paper for a long time. In a nest of mismatched socks on her windowsill, Arthur stirred drowsily and then went back to sleep. She resisted the urge to poke his round body with a pen and tried to concentrate on her letter.

Dear Queen Josephine,

I was very pleased to receive your letter. I am so relieved to know that you and the princesses are in good health. I am sure, as you say, that if I haven't received a letter from my aunt and uncle in the Crownlands it is because of the unreliable postal service, but would appreciate any information about them you might have.

I am in good health, and so is Jilly. Sadly, my uncle Andrew has contracted the Dag, but is still up and around within the confines of his room. We have just consulted with him about going south to help deliver the mail and do other errands.

Errands? That sounded silly, like she was buying ribbons to decorate a new hat. Oh well, Uncle Andrew would be giving more details to the king, via Finn, so Anthea supposed it wasn't all that important. What was important was that she answer the queen's questions.

> I have no wish to cause problems for Dr. Rosemary and her cohorts, but since you asked, I must tell you that I have had little to nothing to do with them since their arrival. They rarely speak to any of us, and they have not expressed any interest in the horses until recently, when Dr. Rosemary asked to take samples of them. She confessed that she had planned to take samples all along, without asking permission or seeking help from the riders. I find this very worrisome. What if they had attempted to take a blood sample from Constantine? He might have killed someone!
>
> Otherwise, I think that they are doing a fine job: we have had only one death so far. It was a hard blow for us, and especially for his horse, Augustus, but we are very lucky that more of us have not succumbed.

Anthea had to pause for a moment. That one death had been very hard. Reynolds, a gentle soul of few words, had been laid to rest the day before, and even the most hardened of the riders had wept. But more distressing was that his horse, Augustus, was still inconsolable. He had had to be heavily restrained and there was talk of sedating him, out of fear that he would hurt himself. How long he would grieve no one was sure. Most riders had died of old age, since they rarely left the farm, and the horses had quietly passed at the same time.

Dr. Rosemary and her people are hard at work on a cure, and taking excellent care of those of the riders who are sick. They have had no cause to deal with the horses, because horses do not get the Dag! That is the best news we have had in some weeks. The horses cannot have caused the disease, because they seem to be immune to it. They cannot spread it, either. We are hoping that this will help people trust horses more, when they see that they are not the cause of the sickness, and that they can be useful!

Dr. Rosemary has proposed that along with delivering messages, we help to gather samples for further study. I am happy that she at last begins to realize our worth, but not pleased at the thought of exposing our riders to more sickness.

All the best wishes to you and your daughters,
Anthea

Anthea quickly sealed the letter into an envelope, stamping the wax with a horseshoe-shaped seal Uncle Andrew had given her for her birthday. She wanted to make sure that she didn't change her mind and go back and start crossing things out and obsessing over every line. She adored the queen, but she was still *the queen*. As it was, Anthea knew she would spend the next several days worrying about how childish "all the best wishes" sounded, or if she should have put her full name underneath.

She addressed the letter, and let herself be pleased with how much her handwriting had improved just in the last year. It was one thing for her old headmistress, Miss Miniver, to tell them to imagine they were writing a letter to the queen, but quite another to know that your letter was actually going to be read by the actual queen. It had done wonders for her handwriting, and Jilly's, though Jilly would never admit it.

But now she had to post the letter, or talk about who was going to post the letter, and that meant an even more frightening task. Before they had even gone up to Andrew's room, Finn had come to her room to present his plan in greater detail. Jilly was with him, but, as Finn said quite bluntly, her vote didn't count.

As soon as he told Anthea why he needed her vote, she understood why Jilly didn't count. She felt much the same way as Jilly, but was a bit more clear-headed about it. Also, she was flattered that Finn had even asked her, since he didn't have to. He was, after all, the King of Leana, though it was only at the farm that they all deferred to him. As far as the Crown was concerned he was a courier like the girls. As far as the Crown was concerned, the Horse Brigade was entirely under the direction of Captain Andrew Thornley and his two lieutenants: Caillin MacRennie and Jack Perkins.

And Perkins was the problem.

It wasn't that Anthea hated Perkins. It wasn't even that Perkins hated Anthea. It was that Perkins hated everyone, and everything, but horses. As little use as he had for other human beings, he especially seemed to have no use for Coronam, and Rose Maidens, and the Crown, and didn't even try to hide his disdain.

With Andrew sick and quarantined, Caillin MacRennie in charge of the entire farm, and Finn too young to be officially in charge, Perkins was the man they had to see. Perkins would need to help them make arrangements and organize routes and riders, supplies and jobs. They knew he would do it, for the good of the brigade. But he definitely wouldn't like some of the details.

"This is beyond foolish," Perkins informed Finn, after they had laid out their plans.

"Here now," Caillin MacRennie countered. "I think it's grand."

Finn had met Anthea and Jilly at the doorway to the dining room, which Caillin MacRennie and Perkins used as an office now. Finn spread out the map and began marking the places in ink where they had tried to establish camps before the Dag, and the places he thought they needed camps with a pencil.

"Beyond foolish. Suicidal," Perkins restated.

"Now, now, think on it," Caillin MacRennie said. "We can make drops and pick-ups without having to touch or speak to another soul. Dr. Rosemary will give us sample boxes with instructions for the local docs, and we won't have to come within twenty feet of the sick.

"It will help us show the people down there in the south our worth."

"We shouldn't have to show them our worth," Perkins said hotly.

"No, we shouldn't," Anthea agreed.

Finn and Jilly turned on her in surprise. She had barely managed to speak in Perkins's presence before, and certainly never agreed with him. Perkins's eyes flickered and then narrowed.

"We shouldn't have to, but nonetheless we need to," Anthea continued. "We need to show people that horses aren't sickly, and that we aren't planning on using them to overthrow the Crown."

"We shouldn't have to," Perkins began again, his pale but not unpleasant features darkening with rage.

"But we *do*," Caillin MacRennie said. "And so we will."

"We haven't even gotten to the bad part yet," Jilly said out of the corner of her mouth.

Anthea put a hand over her eyes. Finn let out a bark of laughter.

"What bad part?" Perkins demanded.

"With so many of the men sick," Finn began, but Perkins had a look of dawning horror on his face before he could finish. "We need as many able-bodied riders—"

"You want to send these little girls south of the Wall to represent us to the south?"

Anthea couldn't decide what part of that sentence was the most insulting, or even what Perkins was trying to say. Did he think they were too young? Too flighty? Too female? Or that the south was too dangerous for them? She decided the whole question offended her.

Jilly clearly felt the same way.

She began to swell like a rare fish that Anthea had once seen at an aquarium in Travertine. Only the fish had been slightly less red in color.

Finn put a hand on Jilly's arm and stopped her. Anthea felt a little pang of jealousy. If she were more prone to loud ranting, she supposed Finn might be holding *her* arm now.

"Are you forgetting, Perkins, that these *little girls* are the ones who took a small herd of horses south, alone, to make peace with King Gareth and forge an alliance with Queen Josephine?"

Perkins's mouth made a fine line. He shook his head.

"And while I know that you dislike the idea of having to have an alliance with the Coronami," Finn said, and Perkins's mouth tightened, "I want you to remember two things: one being that you know very well that the Coronami Crown rules this land whether we like it or not, and two is that if anyone has a reason to complain about that fact, that person should be me."

Even Perkins didn't have a quick reply to that.

Anthea tried and failed at not noticing that Finn had let go of Jilly's arm as soon as he started speaking. She also tried, and succeeded, in sounding supportive without being condescending or gloating toward Perkins as she told Finn, "Jilly and I are ready. We'll go straight to Travertine."

"This is a disaster," Perkins said.

10

THE THEOS

"EVERYBODY LINE UP," ANTHEA shouted. "You get one sad-dlebag of food for yourself, one saddlebag to fill with personal belongings, a bedroll, and two nets of fodder."

"Yes, miss!"

Several of the men shouted it in unison. One of them grumbled, and one of them just turned away to get the things without looking at her. Anthea told herself she didn't care. She didn't need to say these things. They wouldn't forget their food or the fodder for the horses. But it was her job to see off "her" riders, and she would do it whether they liked it or not.

While the men went along the large table set up with sup-plies and filled their saddlebag with sandwiches, cookies, and packets of dried fruit, Anthea turned her attention to the horses. This was the part of her job that she liked. This was the part that the men respected her for as well.

The horses that were about to leave for the south were saddled and bridled and waiting by the nearest fence, right across from the Big House. Anthea moved between the first two stallions and laid a hand on each of their necks. All the men going had the Way, but few of the men had as strong a bond with their horses as she had with Florian. Each of the men would have charge of two horses, but in some cases they had not worked with the second horse before, and that was why Finn had asked Anthea to speak to the horses before they left.

Anthea would have done it anyway, and they both knew it. But he asked, in front of Perkins, and she agreed, in front of Perkins. Perkins, who had in fact managed to persuade Uncle Andrew to keep Anthea and Jilly on the farm, and not send "little girls" out on missions.

Hello, dear friends, Anthea said to the horses. *Are you ready for your adventure?*

They whickered and nodded. The bay on her right moved a little closer to her, and Anthea scratched his neck.

Of course you are, my dears! I am so proud of you! You will do such great things! The Soon King and Constantine are very pleased that you have accepted this job.

The Now King, the bay corrected her.

Yes, you are right, she said ruefully. She hated calling Finn that, since labeling him the soon-to-be-king was as close to treason as she was comfortable with, but some of the horses insisted on it. *The Now King and the herd stallion are very*

*pleased, and they want you to remember to send a message back
to the herd stallion every night, all right?*

They agreed.

*Guard your rider, and follow his orders, but let the herd stal-
lion know if there is anything amiss, all right?*

More agreement, and more neck pats, and then she moved
on to the next pair of horses. But these horses she told to
report to the first pair. They would be farther down the road,
and so their internal voices would be fainter. It would be easier for them to reach the next closest horses than to contact
Constantine.

So Anthea went on down the line, stroking necks and
finger-combing manes, and reminding the horses of the route
they were to take. This group would be going to the west, fol-
lowing the main train line south through Blackham and halfway to Travertine. They would camp within sight of the train
stations and post offices, just outside of any villages, and post
signs with the official seal of the Crown on them, saying that
they were authorized to carry mail and light packages. They
would also need to find the doctors in every town, if they were
alive, and instruct them in collecting samples. Dr. Rosemary
wanted her samples "clean," which meant that whenever possible they needed to be gathered by someone who knew what
they were doing.

They were the third such group to go out, and the first had
gone all the way to Travertine. They had been there a week,

with one camp to the north of the city and another on the east, and four more camps stringing up the highway to the north. So far, so good, and now other groups were being sent out. Few people, other than the royal family, were giving them anything to deliver, but at the very least they were able to relay the news from the capital fairly quickly, though the samples would take longer to deliver.

Not that anyone wanted to hear the news. Most of the news was bad. The weather was cold, even in the south, and the death toll was rising steadily. The king had done his part to spread the word that horses weren't the cause of the illness, but the first reports back from riders indicated that it wasn't that people believed the king so much as they didn't care if they got sick or not, at this point, and so they just ignored the horses while they tried their best to survive.

After Anthea had spoken to all the horses, the men were ready to leave. Finn and Perkins came out of the house and gave a map to the leader of the group, Major Gregory. Gregory, to his credit, was one of the men who had said "Yes, miss!" His group was known as the Theos because his bay stallion was named Theophilus. When the Theos were mounted up they fell into ranks and passed in front of Finn and Perkins, saluting.

When they passed one of the windows at the end of the Big House, they all looked up and saluted again. From his window, Andrew waved. He was on the mend, but still confined to his room. Dr. Rosemary had said that once he had gone two days without coughing or running a fever, he could leave his room. He had not had a fever in a few days, but his cough lingered.

Once the Theos were out of sight down the road, Anthea went to the empty table and began helping the kitchen staff clear away. They had largely been untouched by the Dag, one of the few blessings they could count at the farm. But one of the maids shook her head at Anthea.

"You have enough to do, miss," she said.

Anthea smiled at her and handed over the empty basket she was holding. "I guess that's true," she said.

With the Theos and the two other groups out, that meant that Anthea was one of the last able-bodied riders left at the Last Farm. She had thought that she had a lot to do in the previous weeks, but it was nothing compared to now. A few of the riders had been allowed out of quarantine, which helped, but they were too weak to ride or lift bales of hay or buckets of water.

She got the mares in the paddock to run back and forth, chased by Florian and Leonidas, much to their resentment. Then she jumped the stallions over the fence into another paddock (since Uncle Andrew's curtain was closed now) and chased some of the stallions around. Three riders had died now, and their horses were in mourning. While the other stallions scattered, they stood in the corner of the paddock with their heads down.

Anthea slid off Florian and then sent him after his fellows to keep them moving while she talked to the grief-stricken horses. They gathered around her as soon as her boots hit the ground, pressing her between them. She put her arms over the backs of two of them, and made shushing noises.

Gerard is gone, the big bay stallion, Goliath, said to her.

I know, I know, she told him. *I know, I know*, she told the other two stallions.

One of them, Cassius, had flung himself repeatedly against his stall until his legs were raw and bruised. Now he was swathed in bandages and had moved from a frantic, panicky sort of grief to a numbness that was almost more alarming.

Cassius, how do you feel? Are your legs healing?

Does it matter?

Yes, she assured him. *We all want you to be well again, and strong. We will need you.*

Why?

Soon we will have medicine to fix the Dag. We need to carry medicine to the south so that more people don't die, Anthea said.

She could sense that this pleased Cassius, but not Goliath. Goliath did not care who was saved. His rider hadn't been. Atticus, the third grieving stallion, seemed ready to go either way. They would need to keep an eye on him, more so than the other two, Anthea thought. If they could make Atticus and Cassius excited about going on missions with other riders, Goliath might be won over as well. But if both Atticus and

Goliath refused to work with other riders, the fragile Cassius didn't stand a chance against them.

Anthea made a mental note to tell Finn about their situation, and then headed back toward the Big House. Caillin MacRennie was just riding up from his weekly visit to the village. He exchanged news about what was happening in the north and bought supplies. Before the Dag, the cook and her staff had done it, using the farm's single team of oxen and their high-sided cart. But now that the barely kept secret of the horses was out, and the staff didn't want to risk getting the Dag, Caillin MacRennie had taken over, riding his stallion and leading the oxen.

Now they were headed down the long lane, walled by stone, and Anthea could tell from the slump in Caillin MacRennie's shoulders that the news from Dorling-on-Sea had not been cheerful. Her heart constricted as she thought of dear, plump Mrs. Talbot, maker of the world's finest marzipan. Had she been struck down by the Dag?

Anthea grabbed hold of Florian's saddle as he came over to her and swung herself up. She thought she would trot over and offer some words of comfort to Caillin MacRennie, and get the news, no matter how bad. But as Florian jumped a fence and she could, from his tall back, see over the stone wall to the lane, she kicked him into a gallop.

Something was bobbing along in the wake of the oxcart. Was it an animal? Florian jumped another fence, and Caillin

MacRennie waved his hat at her, although she wasn't sure if he was telling her to slow down or just saying hello. When he noticed that she was aiming Florian at the lane behind him and the cart, however, he reined in his horse and turned to look, putting his hat back on.

It was another hat, a brown knitted hat, that Anthea could see bobbing along in the wake of the cart. A hat worn by a child.

Anthea didn't dare jump Florian over the wall along the lane. He probably could have made it, but the jagged vertical stones at the top made her nervous. Instead she pulled him up alongside it and looked down to see a boy of about eight in a knitted cap gazing back up at her with delight.

"Ar, miss! Is that a horse?"

"Yes . . ."

"Can I have one?"

"Maybe," Anthea said. She leaned down and raised her scarred eyebrow. "But first you have to tell me what you're doing here."

11

A GLIMMER OF HOPE

BEFORE THE BOY COULD answer, Caillin MacRennie waved and shouted for the child to stay in the middle of the drive. "No closer, laddie, if ye please! We've got the Dag here." He smiled as he left the oxen and trotted his horse back toward them. "It's all right, laddie, but stay clear."

The child looked at Anthea and shrugged, but called out, "Yes, sir!" to Caillin MacRennie.

Anthea turned Florian, and Caillin MacRennie came up on the other side of the wall so that they were side by side to survey the child, who stood rocking from foot to foot, his face streaked with dust. He wore a kilt and a felted jacket, like most Leanans, as well as the knitted hat, thick socks, and a scarf against the chilly weather. He had a knapsack on his back, but it was so flat it must have been completely empty.

"What's to do, then?" Caillin MacRennie said.

"We need medicine, sir!"

"Who does?" Caillin MacRennie asked. He looked beyond the child, as though looking for parents. Or any adults, really.

"My village," the boy answered. "Parsiny. It's northwest of here."

"I know it," Caillin MacRennie said. "But what medicine? I'm afraid we're no more better off than any of ye."

"My granddad is a doctor. He says he needs these things." The boy pulled a list out of his pocket. "Willow drops, tansy root." The boy scrunched up his face. "I can't read the rest."

"We'll take care of it," Anthea said. She stretched out a hand and took the paper with her fingertips.

"Did ye walk all the way, my lad?" Caillin MacRennie asked.

"Yes, sir!" the boy answered with real pride.

"Well, sit down on the wall there, and we'll get ye some food." He turned to Anthea, who nodded.

The boy started to protest, and then shrugged and sat down on the bit of grassy bank between the drive and wall. He seemed remarkably unmoved by either the horses or the idea of the Dag being on the farm. Anthea couldn't decide if that meant he was brave or . . . she didn't know what.

She hurried to the stable yard and tied Florian to a ring next to the mounting block. From there she ran straight into the Big House and the kitchen and told the cook what was

happening. Then she went through and into the dining room
to tell Finn and Perkins, who was marking the Theos' path on
a map.

"Parsiny?" Perkins frowned at the map, then tossed it
aside and found one that showed the northern villages. "So it's
not just us."

"Thank heavens," Finn said. "I was worried that we'd
brought it with us when we pulled out of the south." He gave
Anthea a smile, and she smiled back, relieved that she wasn't
the only one who worried about such things.

"It's hardly something to grin about," Perkins said coldly.
"The fact that the Dag can jump the Wall and spread all the
way to the west isn't something to celebrate, in my most hum-
ble opinion."

"And what does this boy want?" Finn asked. "Does he
know we don't have a cure?" He grimaced as he said it.

"It looks like supplies to treat the symptoms," Anthea said.
She held out the paper she had taken from the boy.

"We have all these things, and to spare," Finn said, looking at the note.

"Willow drops? Those we have to spare, but . . ." Perkins
made a mark on the map. "Spreading our men even thinner.
Blast! We hadn't planned to send anyone around the *north*."

"It's not *that* far," Anthea said, studying the map as well.

"A horse could be there and back in a day," Finn agreed.

"Fine, I'll do it," Perkins snapped.

Anthea and Finn goggled at him.

"Why are you looking at me like that?"

"Because you—you—" Finn stammered.

"You never leave the farm and you hate everyone," Anthea said, feeling a blush rise in her cheeks even as she faced Perkins squarely.

Now it was Perkins's turn to goggle.

"I don't hate *everyone*," he said, after too long a pause.

He looked from Anthea to Finn, aghast, but their skeptical expressions didn't change. Finally he shook his head.

"All right. Fine. But the fact remains that we have all the healthy riders in groups and are moving them all out. Finn, you need to stay here with Constantine, because none of the horses are happy about any of this." He swept a hand across the map to indicate the relay teams, the Dag, all of it. "I don't have a team, so—"

"I don't either," Anthea said. "Neither does Jilly."

"I'm not sending a girl out alone to—"

"I am," Finn said. He turned to Anthea. "Would you? Take this boy and some supplies to Parsiny? If you start now you won't be back until after dark, but . . ."

"I'll do it," she said. "I can put the boy on Bluebell, and between her and Florian, we'll be able to carry plenty of things to Parsiny. And after we leave him and the supplies, we'll be able to hurry back."

"Perfect," Finn said, smiling at her.

She felt herself blushing again.

Perkins made a noise in his throat and looked like he was going to argue.

"From this distance," Anthea said coolly, pointing to Parsiny on the map, "if I do run into trouble, I will be able to tell Leonidas, or even Constantine, directly."

"That's impossible," Perkins began. Then he looked at her face, and at Finn's. "It's not impossible, is it?"

They shook their heads in unison. Perkins's face creased, just for a second, and then he was looking back at the map. Anthea felt a sudden surge of pity.

They had never been able to re-create that moment when Florian had sent a plea for help all the way from the south of Coronam to Constantine on the farm, but everyone agreed that Anthea's illness and extreme need had played a part in that. Since Anthea didn't really want to be shot again, and no one else wanted to be shot either to test that theory, they could only practice. Most messages could only be passed through the Way over a handful of miles, which meant that they had to relay them.

But from Parsiny to the farm? From what Anthea and Florian had been able to do running messages in the south, she knew that they could do it easily without needing another horse and rider in between, and that wasn't boasting.

And now Anthea needed to go back to the kitchen and collect the food for the boy, if someone hadn't already run it out to him, but she hesitated. There was something she'd wanted to ask since the Dag had struck Dorling-on-Sea.

"What is it?" Finn asked, seeing her shift from foot to foot.

"I know that the horses didn't cause the Dag, but what did?" Anthea asked. "I mean, how did it get over the Wall? We kept our riders isolated. How do they have it in Dorling-on-Sea, and Parsiny? I asked Dr. Rosemary, but she said she doesn't have time to explain everything to me."

Dr. Rosemary was genuinely trying to include Anthea and even Jilly in her work more. But Anthea suspected that the scientist didn't like admitting that she didn't know things, so her rather vague and extremely technical response to this question made Anthea think that Dr. Rosemary was just as baffled as she was.

"Got to be smugglers," Perkins said shortly.

"Smugglers?" Anthea raised her eyebrows. "You mean exiles trying to sneak back into Coronam?"

Perkins barked a laugh. "Hardly!"

"Actually, a number of ships pass along the coast in both directions," Finn told her. "There are Coronami who enjoy Leanan ale and don't like paying a heavy tax for it, so they pay a smuggler slightly less to bring it south. And many Leanans prefer the Coronami wines to their own ale."

"Oh, dear." Anthea shook her head. "Liquor really is the root of all evil, as Miss Miniver said."

Perkins snorted, and Anthea blushed.

"I'll take some food to the boy," she muttered.

She knew she should be more shocked by the idea of smugglers, but what was the point? Her shock wasn't going to stop the smuggling. And really, weren't they already paying for their illicit activities, now that they had brought the Dag to the north?

She was so caught up in her thoughts that she almost walked right past the little boy, now squatting in the dust. At the last moment, Caillin MacRennie called out and startled her from her reverie. She leaped backward and put the basket on the ground.

"I'll back away, then you come and get it," she told the boy.

"All right, miss," he said, shrugging. "But I've had ring pox."

Ring pox? Anthea thought. *Well, at least they aren't calling it* horse *pox in the north!* She took three steps back and stood by Caillin MacRennie.

"You mean the Dag?" she said.

"Nay, not that, miss," the boy said as he scuttled forward and grabbed a slice of bread out of the basket to cram into his mouth. With his other hand he snatched up the canteen, pulled the cork with his teeth, and gulped half the water at one go. "Ring pox, like most little'uns," he continued when he was done swallowing.

"I don't think we follow ye, laddie," Caillin MacRennie said.

"What's that?" Dr. Hewett came up with a paper in one

hand. Anthea saw that it was the boy's list of supplies, and Dr. Hewett was frowning.

"I was just sayin' as I've had ring pox, and en't gonna get the Dag," the boy said, with a huge, half-chewed mouthful of bread. "So there's no reason t' sit out here." He shrugged again and took another bite. "But if ye insist I do, I guess I do."

Hewett's brows pulled together.

"Are you saying," he asked carefully, "that because you've had ring pox you can't get the Dag?"

"That's right," the boy said back, dust-streaked face cheerful as he polished off the bread and discovered a large green apple in the basket.

"Who told you that?"

"My granddad. He's a doctor." The boy's cheerful face clouded. "He's awful sick now, can I bring him medicine?"

Other people were starting to wander over to observe this strange conference on the front drive. Dr. Rosemary came out of nowhere, seemingly, and tapped Anthea's shoulder. Anthea jumped about a foot in the air.

"Did that boy say something about ring pox?" Dr. Rosemary asked when Anthea hit the ground. "Is that making the rounds as well?"

"I've had ring pox," Anthea said.

"I shouldn't worry about it, then, you only get it once," Dr. Rosemary said brusquely. "Hewett, where do you get your needles from?" She was studying a list as well.

"Dr. Rosemary," Hewett said in a strangled voice.

"I've had ring pox," Anthea repeated, louder. "Jilly's had it, right?"

"She did have it," Dr. Hewett said, turning from studying the boy. "You and Jillian had it at the same time. I was still a rider then." He grimaced. "But I remember you sneaking out to play with the foals even though you were both bright red with the fever rash."

"Oh, aye," Caillin MacRennie said suddenly. "Coughed so hard she fell on her face in the mud." He pointed to Anthea, who felt her cheeks turn red. "I carried you both back into the house like sacks of misbehaving potatoes."

"And the horses are inoculated against it, aren't they?" Anthea said.

She had helped Dr. Hewett and Uncle Andrew inoculate the new foals in the spring. Inoculation was relatively new, but Dr. Hewett was a staunch supporter of it.

"Wait, what did you all just say?" Dr. Rosemary looked up from her list.

"The boy says his granddad—his grandfather, I mean—told him that he couldn't get the Dag, since he'd already had ring pox."

Dr. Rosemary didn't reply, and as the boy was busy with his apple, Anthea turned to look at her. The scientist was standing with her mouth open, one hand poised halfway to her throat. The scientist continued to stare over Anthea's shoulder for a heartbeat or two, then she slowly focused on Anthea's face. She reached out and touched Anthea's chin, turning her face from side to side, examining Anthea with her sharp eyes.

"You've had no symptoms of the Dag?"

"No, ma'am."

"I had a mild case of ring pox," Dr. Hewett said. "And practiced inoculation on myself in medical college as well." He held out his arms to show that he had no symptoms of the Dag.

"I need a list of all the members of the brigade who have had ring pox," Dr. Rosemary said, intense. She looked around. "But none of the horses have gotten it?"

"Ring pox?" Dr. Hewett said. "Or the Dag?"

"I *know* they haven't gotten the Dag," Dr. Rosemary said irritably. "But what about ring pox? Do they get that?"

"They could, but we inoculate them," Hewett said.

"I helped," Anthea said. "With the foals. In the spring."

Both doctors turned to look at her. The boy had moved closer, and was standing beside Anthea, both of them staring at Hewett and Dr. Rosemary.

Dr. Hewett looked at Dr. Rosemary. "Jacoby, the surgeon here before me, inoculated all the horses, and I've carried on. We're on the second generation of horses who have been inoculated."

"We need to check the riders," Dr. Rosemary said. They were nodding at each other, as though sharing a secret.

"Finn's had ring pox," Anthea said. Everyone looked at her. "He has a scar on his wrist," she mumbled, turning red. "So they're related, ring pox and the Dag?"

"My granddad says they are," piped up the boy.

Anthea started to shush him, but Dr. Rosemary held up a finger, and began lecturing.

"Ring pox," she said, "causes a widespread rash dotted with small blisters, and a hacking cough." She held up another finger. "The Dag causes fever, rashy spots with occasional blisters, and a hacking cough." She pointed to herself, then Anthea. "I've had ring pox, this girl has had ring pox, that boy has had ring pox, and none of us has gotten the Dag."

Dr. Hewett nodded again.

"Go to the stable," he instructed Anthea. "Ask any men you find. I'll check with the ill."

Anthea ran to the stable, and surprised a group of riders coming out of it. She held out her arms to stop them in the door of the stable.

"Have any of you had ring pox?"

"What?" The leader of the group, a grizzled man Anthea didn't know that well, just stared at her. "Ring pox?"

"Yes, please! As children, perhaps?"

"Oh, blimey! There's another epidemic on?" One of the men spit in the dirt with disgust.

"Just answer the question," Anthea shouted, stamping her foot.

The graying man said, "All right! I've had it!" He showed her a small round scar on his left forearm, like a tiny white dot in the otherwise tanned (and rather hairy) skin.

"Me too!" The spitter raised a hand, and so did the other six men.

"You've all had it?"

"Yes, miss," they chorused.

"Thank you!"

She pushed between their horses and went into the stable. Halfway down the first row of stalls, she found Keth sitting on an overturned bucket. She marched up to him, but couldn't get his attention until she snapped her fingers in his face.

"Have you had ring pox?"

He raised his head to look up her. He looked awful: his eyes were red and swollen, his nose was streaming, and there were tears pouring down his cheeks even as he gaped at her.

"What's wrong?" She drew back in alarm.

"My mum," he said thickly. "She's got it. The Dag. They won't let me see her."

"Oh, no."

Anthea adored Nurse Shannon, they all did. And Keth's father had died a long while back; it was only he and his mother in their little cottage behind the Big House. Anthea put a hand on his shoulder and squeezed.

"But we . . . there might be good news," she ventured.

"What do you mean?" He blew his nose loudly.

Anthea handed him her handkerchief for good measure. "We just . . . there's a little boy . . ." She realized she didn't want to give him false hope. "I wondered if you've had ring pox?"

He looked confused, but he answered. "Yeah. I was eleven. Real bad. I've got pocks all over my back."

"Oh, good!"

He stared at her through bleary eyes. "What does it mean?"

Anthea stood up. "It means you can't get the Dag. They think."

His eyes narrowed. "But I've had a cough for weeks."

"That cough," Anthea said slowly. "The cough, but no rash, right?"

He nodded.

"Go, tell Dr. Rosemary. Right now!"

"What about my mum? Will it help?" He jumped to his feet.

"This *is* helping!" she called over her shoulder as she hurried out.

After questioning all the riders she could find, Anthea met up with Caillin MacRennie and the young boy in the dining room. They also had Finn, Perkins, and Drs. Hewett and Rosemary, all in a high state of excitement. They compared notes, and it seemed that all the healthy members of the brigade had suffered ring pox as children. Uncle Andrew had experienced a very mild case as an adult, when Jilly and Anthea had gotten it.

"All this time, Keth has probably had the Dag, but not been sick," Dr. Hewett said, his brow clouded. "Why did we never take samples from him before?" He shook his head. "We've been fools, stumbling in the dark," he muttered.

"But now the light has come," Dr. Rosemary said. Her eyes were wide and shining. "The two must be related, strains of the same master disease!" She seized Dr. Hewett by the shoulders. "Do you know what this means?"

"What *does* it mean?" It was Anthea who asked, echoed by Jilly.

"What does what mean, and why are you all running around?" Jilly clarified, coming all the way into the room. "And why am I the only one exercising the nine thousand horses out there?" She narrowed her eyes at Anthea.

Dr. Rosemary looked at her with the first hint of a real smile that Anthea had ever seen the woman have. "It means, Miss Jillian, that you are immune to the Dag."

12

YOUNG TIM AND SIR TIMOTHY

"WHY DO YOU WANT to go to Bellair?"

The boy from Parsiny, whose name was Tim, was full of questions. Most of them were about horses, which he was not at all afraid of but found completely fascinating. In point of fact, he was riding one, and doing better than Anthea had on her first day.

"Because," was her only reply to this latest question. "Sit up straight, shoulders back."

"*Because* en't an answer," the boy said.

Anthea gave him a quelling look.

Anthea was riding Florian and leading Goldenrod, who was laden with baskets of medicine, the ring pox inoculation, syringes, rubbing alcohol, and instructions. Dr. Hewett had showed Anthea his letter, which admitted that he had mostly inoculated horses, but since it seemed to be working on him, they should give it a try. Meanwhile, Dr. Rosemary got to work on a specific inoculation against the Dag, using the one for ring pox as a recipe.

Tim, perched atop Campanula, now began to whistle. Loudly. No wonder Bluebell had decided carrying the child was beneath her dignity.

This was not the way Anthea had pictured her first real mission as a member of the brigade. She had imagined thundering up the road, skidding into the village square and holding aloft a saddlebag of medicine to a grateful populace. But between Tim and the heavy packs on Goldenrod, they could hardly move at a trot, let alone a gallop.

"But if this goes well, they're going to need inoculations at Bell Hyde," she murmured.

"Did you say something about Bellair again?" Tim's chirping voice interrupted her thoughts. "Why would you go there? Isn't it south of the Wall? Aren't there even *more* sick people there? They don't like horses, you know." He shook his head over this.

"They need medicine," Anthea said tartly. "There are many sick people there. And some of them are family. My family. My friends."

"So your mother and father are there? In Bellair?" Tim would not be deterred.

"My father is dead. My mother lives . . . very far away."

"Both my parents are dead," he said. "They died when I was a baby. My nurse put me on a train with a note for my granddad when I was a year old. Granddad's lived here for ages." He took up his whistling again.

That caught Anthea's attention. "So you were born in Coronam?"

"Yep. So was Granddad. 'Cept the king didn't like him, so he moved up here."

"What? What do you mean?"

But a squirrel had caught young Tim's attention, and it took a moment for Anthea to drag him back to the conversation.

"I was born in Camryn," Tim continued when they'd lost sight of the squirrel. "Have you ever been to Camryn?"

"Yes," Anthea said. "They are well known for their sheep, and the castle is one of the oldest structures in Coronam."

"Uh-huh," Tim said. "My father worked in the castle. He used to lead people around, show them *the dungeons*," Tim dropped his voice to make it sound spooky. "My granddad was the doctor in a village right by there," he went on in his usual cheerful tone, "and his best friend was in charge of all the old books and stuff in the castle and the village. I think. No one ever tells me the name of the village."

"Oh," Anthea said. "That's nice, about the castle."

They were coming to a crossroads, and she steered Florian down the left-hand road. According to the signpost, they were only three miles from Parsiny.

"Then my granddad's friend, he read something in the old books about the Royal Family, and he showed Granddad, and

they showed the king. And that's why the king killed Granddad's friend, and Granddad had to move here."

"What?" Anthea pulled up Florian.

Beloved? What is wrong?

"The king," Tim repeated. "He didn't like the books they
found. So he burned them. Then he killed Granddad's friend,
and told Granddad he could come here or die, too."

Anthea was aghast. Who had told the child such a terrible
story? His grandfather? Perhaps this was his way of covering
up his true crime to spare his grandson's feelings.

"You shouldn't say such things," Anthea told him.

The boy shrugged. "We're almost there!" He spurred
Campanula into a jog.

Anthea followed at a walk for a while, but when she saw
the village ahead, she stepped up the pace. She was tired, but
she took a moment to wonder if she should explain the Way to
Tim, and find out if he had it.

They reached the well in the middle of the village square,
and halted the horses. There was a small stone church, a
store, a school, and several other buildings. A dog barked at
the horses, and Arthur poked his head out of Anthea's jacket
to snap his beak at the dog, which ran off.

"Where is everyone?" Anthea shifted uneasily in her
saddle. Florian, sensing her nervousness, stopped lipping the
bucket on the side of the well and laid back his ears.

"They're sick," the boy said, as though talking to a

simpleton. He slithered down from Campanula's back, as neatly as if he'd been doing it for years. He pointed to a squat stone building on the left. "That's Granddad's surgery."

Anthea dismounted, trying to be as graceful as Tim and almost succeeding. She tied the horses to a post near a communal trough.

Tim, meanwhile, had run to the surgery. Anthea hoped he wasn't going to try and rouse his grandfather from his sickbed. She had no desire to meet the exile. She unloaded the supplies, lining them up on the green where they would be easy to find. She had the feeling that people were watching her from behind their curtains, but shook it off.

"And here she is!" Tim came out of the clinic and pointed eagerly at Anthea.

With him was a woman, not his grandfather, Anthea saw with relief. She was young, no more than thirty, and wore a neat brown skirt and pale blue blouse. She smiled warmly at Anthea.

"How d'ye do, miss?" The woman crossed the green with light steps and held out a hand to Anthea.

"Very well, thank you," Anthea said automatically. She shook the offered hand, a little nervously despite her leather gloves.

"You've brought us medicine?" The woman's eyes lit on the parcels.

"Yes, and instructions for administering inoculations. Though if you've had ring pox, you won't need it," Anthea said.

She was aware that she was babbling, but she hadn't really thought about what to say. "Tim told us the connection."

The woman looked at her in astonishment. "Oh, did ye not know that? Sir Timothy says they're one and the same, really."

"Sir Timothy?"

"Aye, young Tim's granddad," the woman said. She jerked her head back at the clinic. "Quite ill, poor soul. Nursed half the town until he fell ill himself."

"That's a shame," Anthea said. She lowered her voice, watching Tim as he prodded a box of blister ointment. "Will Sir Timothy . . . pull through?"

"Most likely. He's a tough old nut," the woman said.

"Do you think he might be well enough to help take some samples? We are trying to formulate a more specific cure for the Dag," Anthea said, throwing her shoulders back.

"Oh, my! I'm sure I can help with that if Sir Timothy isn't up to it," the woman said, beaming. "I'm Mary Jones, by the way. I teach Tim and the other young folk."

"I'm Anthea . . . er, I'm Anthea," Anthea said, deciding not to toss around her family name.

"Thank you, Anthea. And thank your captain, as well. It's wonderful of you horse-riders to deliver medicine this way."

"You're welcome," Anthea said. She looked at Mary curiously. "Are you really not afraid of horses?"

"Oh, of course not!" Mary laughed. "We know better than to believe those old superstitions!"

"Er, quite," Anthea said.

"Which superstitions?"

A large man with rumpled white hair limped out of the office, leaning heavily on a cane. He coughed into a handkerchief and looked around with watering eyes.

"Granddad, this is Anthea!" Tim ran up to throw an arm around the old man's waist. He gestured extravagantly at Anthea, as though he had conjured her from thin air. "And those are three of her horses!"

"They're not *my* horses," Anthea muttered, trying not to be rude and step back from the man who was both very ill and an exile. "Well, not all of them."

Florian had grunted and flipped his ears at her when she said they weren't hers. Goldenrod, however, bobbed her head up and down in agreement.

"They look to be fine beasts," he said, but he was looking at Anthea more than the horses. His eyes, now that the tears brought on by his cough had cleared, were a sharp green that seemed to see right through Anthea. "And you're Anthea, you said? Anthea what?"

"Just Anthea is fine, sir," she said.

"You look very familiar," he said.

Before Anthea could think of a reply, Tim decided he couldn't wait any longer.

"She has the *Way*, Granddad! She must be a *real Leanan*! I always thought they'd look different, but she just looks the same as anybody!"

He danced around his grandfather like a trained monkey.

Anthea wondered if, like a monkey, he would be quiet if she gave him a biscuit.

Sir Timothy scrutinized Anthea. "The Way? And you're Leanan? But I could swear . . . How did they find you?"

"I really must go," Anthea said. "I need to get back to the farm."

But the old man was still keenly interested in her. "I'll wager you didn't volunteer," he said. "Thrown into it by virtue of having the Way. But how did they *find* you?" He squinted at Anthea. "The Thornleys are lucky your family didn't raise a protest, haul you back over the Wall by your hair." He paused, and his eyes caught on the rose pendant pinned to Anthea's coat. "A Rose Maiden, eh?"

"I'm Anthea Thornley," Anthea said. "Andrew Thornley's niece."

Sir Timothy's eyes went wide, and he went into a fit of coughing that nearly made him fall. Mary and Tim both rushed to prop him up and pound on his back, while Anthea dithered helplessly. Should she . . . what? She had no idea.

What is wrong? Florian asked. *Should we go?*

I don't know! I don't understand, she wailed mentally in response. *I thought he knew Uncle Andrew! Why is he so upset that I'm Uncle Andrew's niece?*

"Genevia Cross-Thornley," Sir Timothy gasped out when he had stopped coughing. Tim was trying to pull his grandfather back inside, but the old man shook him off gently. "You're Genevia Cross-Thornley's daughter."

It was not a question, but Anthea nodded anyway. Her heart was stuttering in her chest. She had no doubt that he knew her mother, she could see it on his face. Knew her, and didn't like her. How to tell Sir Timothy that the dislike was mutual?

Not that it's any of his business, she thought to Florian. She lifted her chin.

"Your mother," Sir Timothy grated out. "Your *mother*."

Anthea started backing toward Florian. She wished she hadn't tied him quite so tightly.

"Did she send you to spy on your uncle? Convenient that you also have the Way." He stopped to cough. "Unless she cast you out for having it. Nothing would surprise me."

"Sir Timothy," Mary said in shock. "You are unwell!"

"Your mother, the spy, the book burner, the murderess," Sir Timothy began to rant. "She's the reason I'm here! She's the reason Tim is here, and an orphan!" He pointed a gnarled and shaking finger at Anthea.

"I didn't know," Anthea gasped out. She kept backing toward Florian. "I thought she was dead!"

Tears sprang to her eyes. Florian was yanking on his reins, trying to pull free. Why, oh why didn't she remember to only tie him with a slipknot? Anthea thought frantically as she tried to get his reins loose.

Tim was staring at Anthea as though she were a monster.

"That's the lady you told me about?" He pulled at his grandfather's arm. "The one who wanted you to die? Her mum?"

"No," Anthea whispered.

"Ask your uncle," Sir Timothy said roughly. "Ask yourself, where this illness started, and where your mother was when it did."

"What?" Anthea froze.

"You think it was coincidence that the newspapers reported horses outside of Travertine, and then a month later, an epidemic comes sweeping out of that same place?"

Anthea had finally gotten the reins untied. She was on Florian's back and had a hold of Campanula and Goldenrod before she even registered it.

Let's go, Florian urged.

I don't like that man, Campanula announced. She pranced and tossed her head. *I liked the boy. But I want to leave. Now.*

"The instructions for gathering samples are in that packet," Anthea said. "We'll send someone else to collect them in a few days." She sucked in a deep breath. "When Tim is older, send him to the Last Farm, he might have the Way."

She turned Florian and they fled.

FLORIAN

Florian did not like the turmoil in Beloved Anthea's mind. He did not like the stiff way she sat in the saddle, or the muddiness of her thoughts.

That man, the man with the cane, had said something to her. Something about That Woman Her Mother, the one who smelled of dying roses. Florian had not been paying attention, for which he blamed himself. The Boy Called Tim had been a cheerful young companion, with nosings of the Way, and so Florian did not see a threat in the Boy Called Tim's home.

But the old man with the cane had been a threat. He had said things to Beloved Anthea that disturbed her. She had left without checking that he and the mares drank enough water, had not given them food, which was most unlike her. She would not talk all the way back home, and though Florian left her to her silence, he did not like it.

They returned to find Last Farm in an uproar. Alarmed, Florian called to Constantine to ask what he should do, should he take Beloved Anthea and the mares far from here?

No, came Constantine's answer. The men were elated and had found a cure for this coughing sickness that plagued them. The Thornley was released from his exile, and moved among them again, and the lights and candles were not a sign of danger, but of their hard work making more medicine despite the lateness of the hour.

She Who Was Jilly came toward them, all laughter and smiles, but Beloved Anthea did not reply. She got down from Florian's back, and then Florian did not know what to do.

Beloved Anthea gave his reins to She Who Was Jilly.

You must take care of them, Beloved Anthea told She Who Was Jilly, and walked away from Florian and the mares.

What are you doing? She Who Was Jilly demanded, and it was echoed by Florian's thoughts.

I have to write a letter to the queen, Beloved Anthea said. She did not look back.

13

MAJOR GREGORY RETURNS

ANTHEA WOULD HAVE WORRIED about how long it took for the queen to answer her letter, but she was far too busy.

Dr. Rosemary and the other scientists were manufacturing the vaccine as fast as they could. They tested it on the riders who were sick, to see if it could heal as well as prevent the disease. It was too early to tell, Dr. Rosemary said, but none of the ingredients could hurt them.

Keth was anxious for them to give it to his mother. Nurse Shannon had gotten steadily sicker, and he confided to Anthea that he was worried it was his fault.

"How could that be?" Anthea asked when he told her this.

They were in the stables, the horses tied in the aisles so that they could go down the line and groom them all. Anthea had Florian and Campanula at the end, so that she could do them last and spend more time on them. They had been very upset with her after the trip to Parsiny, and she was still apologizing a week later.

She finished up with Castor and moved on to his twin, Pollux. Keth coughed and moved to poor Hercules, whose rider had died three days earlier.

"Because of that," Keth said, pointing to his mouth and coughing again. "This stupid cough! I should have been put in quarantine immediately! Instead I kept on sleeping in our tiny cottage and letting my mum take care of me!"

"I thought they tested you, and it wasn't the Dag," Anthea said. She did her best not to take an involuntary step back, all the same.

"Yeah, but a week ago they didn't know the Dag and ring pox were the same, either," Keth said.

"But your mother definitely has the Dag," Anthea argued.

She had helped Dr. Rosemary sort the samples taken from the riders and other residents of the farm just the day before. Two of the riders actually had pneumonia from riding too hard in wet weather, and not the Dag at all, and had been moved to one of the cottages to be treated by Dr. Hewett.

"You've had the Dag," Anthea pointed out. "Well, its cousin anyway. You made me look at the scars on your shoulder."

It had become like a secret society around the farm. Those who had had ring pox had taken to flashing their scars at each other, which made Anthea highly uncomfortable. She had never seen so many men's stomachs, and had actually happened upon Keth and Finn comparing scars in the stable. Both of them had been shirtless, and while Keth was rather gangly, Finn most certainly was not, and Anthea had been caught staring at the muscles of his back and shoulders, and then run off, blushing furiously.

"But how do they *know*?" Keth said.

"They know," she said firmly. "These are some of the finest scientists in Coronam. They have been studying the Dag for months, using all the newest methods. Your mother will be just fine. You'll see."

Keth relaxed a little, nodding his head, and Anthea patted him on the shoulder the way she would a horse.

Jilly came in from taking her turn with the scientists, and grabbed a brush and comb from a bucket of supplies. Anthea and Keth had left Caesar and Buttercup for her, but she went over to Pollux.

"You'd better do Florian," she said under her breath. "I can tell he's still upset."

After giving Pollux a final pat on the rump, Anthea moved down the line to Florian. He was standing with his head down, his tail and ears limp. Anthea put the brush on the top of a half door and put her arms around his neck.

My love, my love, she whispered to him. *My love, my love, forgive me.*

It had been a week, and Anthea had asked Florian to

forgive her every day. He said that he was not angry with her, but something was clearly still wrong. Bluebell had nipped at Anthea's hair, but then she had settled down to her usual self, and Goldenrod and Campanula had acted as though there was nothing to forgive. But something was still wrong with Florian.

You must tell me, darling, Anthea said, picking up the brush and beginning to sweep it down his shoulder. *What is wrong?*

That man upset you, Florian said.

And I am sorry that I was too upset to take care of you, Anthea replied. *But I am all right now.*

You are not all right, Florian countered. *You are still upset, my beloved. And . . . and there are others. Something is not right.*

A thrill of fear went through Anthea. Beyond Florian, Bluebell and Leonidas whickered and stamped.

What do you mean? What isn't right? Anthea stopped brushing. *Tell me!*

Something is very wrong, Florian said. *But I . . . Theophilus!*

"What?" Anthea said aloud.

"What?" Jilly called out to her. "Did you say something?"

"Theophilus?"

"Gregory and Theo are supposed to stay at their posting," Keth said. "He won't be back for weeks."

Anthea paused. She remembered sending Major Gregory and Theophilus and his group, the Theos, off. She reached out now, with the Way, looking for one of the horses from that group.

Theophilus was coming up the road, but she couldn't find any of the others. Anthea slipped Florian's lead free of the ring on the wall and gave a little tug, but he didn't need it. They walked quickly out of the stable together, and then Anthea scrambled up onto his back so that she could see over the fences.

Theophilus came down the lane at a quick walk, with Gregory hunched over his neck. It looked like the major was tired, and no wonder. He had been positioned the farthest south of any of the riders, and if he had ridden straight back, both horse and rider must be exhausted. Anthea saw that Theophilus had a little hitch to his walk. She couldn't believe that Major Gregory would keep going if his horse was lame, but maybe he really was asleep in the saddle.

Florian went rigid. He was facing into the wind, and he suddenly pointed with his nose toward Theophilus and his rider.

Blood. This is what is wrong.

Anthea urged the reluctant Florian forward until she could see Theophilus clearly. He was dark with sweat, his eyes visibly white-rimmed, and Gregory was slumped on his back like he was going to fall off at any moment. He wasn't asleep, he was . . . gray.

Blood, came the impression from the horses in the nearest paddock. The iron tang of it filled Anthea's nostrils as the stench reached the horses. At the center of the farm in his private field, Constantine reared onto his hind legs and screamed.

Anthea leaped down from Florian's back and ducked out of the paddock. She hurried to Major Gregory, along with everyone else around who had the Way. They must have all gotten the same impression from the horses. When she reached Theophilus's side and caught his reins, she saw that Gregory's left side was dark and slick with blood.

"Major Gregory! Major Gregory!"

Anthea held the reins in her left hand and shook the man with her right. To her relief, Gregory groaned and tried to straighten up.

"Hold on, I've got you," she told him, and began leading Theophilus toward the barn where all the doctors were working.

Caillin MacRennie came charging onto the scene, took one look at the blood coating Gregory's uniform, and took command.

"Get the surgeon! Get Hewett, I say!" he shouted.

He reached for Theophilus's reins, and Anthea was more than willing to give them up, but Theophilus pulled away, and a clear impression of Anthea struck them both. It seemed that, distressed, the horse preferred the familiar touch of the girl who gave him carrots to the loud man shouting for a surgeon.

Hewett came limping out of the barn, his face already grim with concern. One of the scientists trailed behind him, still holding out a vial that he had been working with, but he shook his head at her and pointed to Theophilus. Anthea saw the woman's mouth form an O, and she ducked back inside.

Hewett rolled up to them with his bent-legged gait and grabbed at Gregory's coat. The heavy wool parted, and Anthea nearly fainted at the sight of the flesh underneath: bruised, bloodied, and with a large round hole that seeped more blood with every one of the major's breaths. The blood looked dark and thick, and Anthea wondered if that meant something. Something bad.

"Shot," Hewett announced. "Some filthy old musket, by the size of that hole. Get him down and into my house."

Hewett's house was one of the little stone cottages next to the Big House. When they reached it Finn was suddenly at her elbow, taking the reins from her. Theophilus didn't seem to mind Finn, so she gave them up, and was wondering what to do with herself as two men dragged the unconscious and bloodied Major Gregory off the stallion's back.

Good boy, Anthea said to Theophilus. *Thank you for bringing the major home.*

"Come along," Hewett barked, and after a moment Anthea realized that he was talking to her. "I need assistance."

The front room of the cottage was dominated by a long worktable, scrubbed pale and holding several books and a large candelabrum, since the only gaslights at the farm were in the main house. Dr. Hewett swept the books onto a chair and put the candelabrum on top of a china dresser in the corner.

"Lay him there," he ordered the men carrying Gregory. He stuck his head back out of the door. "Make sure that poor Theophilus gets the care he needs. Brave lad," he said under his breath as he turned around. "Somebody light the candles." He waved at the box of matches, and Anthea hurried to light the candelabrum and any other lamps she could find.

Carefully the men stretched Gregory out on the table, which was exactly the right length. Gregory gasped a little, and his eyelids fluttered, making Anthea cringe. She wondered how much pain he was in: Would he start screaming or thrashing about? She didn't know if she could maintain her poise in such circumstances. She barely remembered her own injury and recovery from the year before; she had never been good around sick people or blood.

"Theo?" Gregory whispered.

"He's fine," Anthea whispered back. "He brought you safely home, and he's about to have extra oats and a nice rubdown."

"The scissors, Miss Thea, just there," Hewett said as he washed his hands in a basin of water. He pointed to a heavy pair of shears on a side table. "Use them."

"Use them to *what*?" Anthea went to the scissors, but didn't pick them up.

"To cut off his coat," the surgeon said.

"Um," Anthea said.

"Come on now," Dr. Hewett said. "I thought Rose Maidens were supposed to soothe fevered brows?"

"This isn't—"

"You faced down Constantine, you can do this!"

Anthea closed her mouth, took the scissors in shaking hands, and went to Gregory's side. He moaned as she began to gingerly cut through the blood-saturated wool of his coat. His eyes fluttered open and he stared at her as though he had never seen her before.

"Major?" Her voice was barely a whisper. She asked the question that had been on her lips since she'd seen the blood. "Who shot you?"

For a moment she thought he wasn't capable of answering. His eyes closed, and his grayish lips moved without making any sound. Then his voice, thin and thready, followed.

"*They* did."

"Who did?"

"The people."

"What people, Major?" She leaned in close.

Beyond the injured man she could see Dr. Hewett filling a syringe with something . . . morphine probably. His face was twisted in a cynical expression that said he already knew the answer.

"The people in the village. Threw the medicine in the midden. 'Horse-tainted,' they said. Tried to get it back . . . tried to . . . save it. Shot me."

The scissors dropped to the tabletop with a clatter. Now Anthea felt her own mouth stiffen into an O. She looked from the major, who had slipped into unconsciousness, to the surgeon, who stepped forward to give the wounded man the shot.

Dr. Hewett looked at Anthea's pale face and smiled grimly.

"You didn't honestly think that people were using the medicine, did you? You know what they're like better than any of us. They'd rather die than touch anything 'horse-tainted.'"

"But we can stop the Dag!" Anthea sputtered. "We can stop people from dying!"

"None of that matters if you trot into town on the back of a horse."

"They shot him," Anthea said later, for what was probably the hundredth time.

Her uncle handed her a glass, and she tossed back the water like it was whiskey and slammed the glass down on the table for emphasis.

"They shot him," she choked out. "And he was delivering medicine for their children!"

Through watery eyes she saw Caillin MacRennie and her uncle exchange glances. Jilly, lounging in a chair nearby, perked up, clearly sensing a secret. Even Perkins stopped drawing maps to look at her uncle, expectant.

"Everyone deserves to know the truth," Caillin MacRennie said. "The lasses should know what's becoming of our work."

"What *is* becoming of our work?" Jilly was on her feet now. She prowled over to the table to stand at Anthea's shoulder.

"We reckon that over half of the medicine and supplies we drop off goes unused," Uncle Andrew said bluntly. "Some places don't even let us drop it. They chase our men away, threatening them if they leave so much as an eyelash on the road, let alone a package." He sighed.

"I'm sure Dr. Rosemary can wave her samples goodbye. I wondered if we should wait for the king to make an official announcement . . . but Queen Josephine's letter arrived first, and she gave us the go-ahead . . ." He smiled faintly. "She wants to believe people will get used to horses as badly as we all do, but I just don't think it's going to happen."

"But they're wearing *uniforms*," Anthea said.

"It doesn't matter, Thea," Uncle Andrew said. "Think of how you felt when you first came here. The Coronami fear horses far too much."

"The king has done his work well," Perkins said bitterly.

"What do you mean?" Anthea said. "He's made announcements, he's trusted us to deliver coded messages! He is just too sick to make an official statement about the medicine . . ."

She trailed off, seeing Perkins shake his head, and Uncle Andrew and Caillin MacRennie exchange looks.

"Sandwich teapot bunny slippers?" Perkins said with a sneer. "Biscuit dragon turnip stew? Those weren't real messages. They were just a big test. Which we failed."

"What?" Jilly screamed it in Anthea's ear.

Anthea was too shocked to do more than slide sideways in her chair, however. Jilly used this as an invitation to cram herself into the seat next to Anthea, one arm squeezing her cousin's neck.

"What are you talking about?" Jilly demanded.

"You think I hate everyone," Perkins said. "And you might be right. But it's with good reason." He picked up some papers on the table and rolled them into a tube, smacking it into his palm over and over again.

"The king wanted to make sure that we were reliable, and to test our speed and accuracy and all those things," Uncle Andrew said before Perkins could open his mouth to release what was sure to be a violent rant.

"Which we knew," he added pointedly. "What we didn't learn until very recently was that it was *all* a test. We never were given any real messages. And the king decided after only a week that the cost of feeding riders and horses was greater than our usefulness."

"A week?" Anthea was aghast. "We were living rough for *months!*"

"I bet the queen made him keep us working," Jilly said dully.

"Yes," Uncle Andrew said shortly. "Josephine hoped that he would come around eventually. But I don't think he has. I think he's pretending to be sick, or too busy, to answer my letters now, which is why I didn't wait to begin distributing medicine."

"Now I hate everyone, too," Jilly said to Perkins.

"Except the queen," Anthea said, loosening her cousin's grip on her neck.

"Except her."

"I had no idea they would hate us so much they would refuse medicine," Anthea went on. "That's . . . insane."

"It's not so much the medicine as the way of it," Caillin MacRennie said. "The vaccines are so new . . . people are wary of it. Don't like needles." He shrugged. "Then somebody on a horse rolls up, with a bag of needles, says they want your blood in exchange for medicine that takes more pokes and prods to give out . . . well!"

"I still hate everyone but the queen," Jilly said.

"And me," Anthea said.

"And you. And everyone in this room."

"Do you think Major Gregory will be all right?" Anthea had to change the subject. It was just too depressing to think of all the time and medicine and work wasted. "I think that was worse than the time I got shot."

"If he doesn't get an infection, he'll be fine," her uncle said.

"A collapsed lung," Perkins broke in. "A smashed rib—"

"He'll be fine," Andrew repeated.

"There's no sense coddling them, Commander," Perkins continued, with a look on his face like a man prodding a bear with a stick.

"I'm not coddling them," Uncle Andrew said in icy tones. "I'm coddling *myself*. Trying to convince myself that my life's work hasn't been completely in vain. That the people of Coronam aren't going to try and kill us when we're attempting to save their lives."

"It'll take the southerners a while to get used to us," Caillin MacRennie said in an attempt to soothe Uncle Andrew.

"Speaking of southerners," Perkins said, even gloomier.

"Shut yer flap," Caillin MacRennie barked at the man.

"Kronenhof? Are we at war?" Jilly's face was puckered with worry.

"Is it happening?" Anthea's voice squeaked.

"Possibly," Uncle Andrew said.

"The horses, on a battlefield?" Anthea felt her stomach drop.

"You know that they've been trained," her uncle reminded her.

"If Florian . . . any of them . . . were killed." Anthea could barely say it.

"Don't worry," Perkins said. "People won't take medicine from us, they're not going to let us fight."

"It does seem unlikely that Gareth would send us to war," Uncle Andrew said

"We're finally at war?" Finn came into the room, holding a letter in his hand.

"No," Andrew said.

"We should be so lucky," Jilly chimed in. Anthea jabbed her with an elbow.

"Ow!"

"That's not *lucky*," Anthea whispered.

"Um, all right," Finn said, confused. "I just . . . I have something I need to do first."

"What is it?" Andrew said.

"It's from the queen," Finn explained. "She wants me to carry medicine personally to her home village.

"Her *real* home village."

14

THE SHEPHERD'S HUT

ANTHEA WRAPPED HER LONG coat around her tightly. Snow was falling, and the treeless stretches of the West Country had allowed the wind to whip the earlier snows into a sculpted landscape like a rumpled linen sheet. It had been icy cold, but the snow was somehow warmer, which made Anthea deeply suspicious. She had heard that before you froze to death, you felt warm again. She didn't think it had reached that point yet, but it was surely just a matter of time.

They were in the middle of nowhere, in the winter, and Anthea had volunteered to stay there alone. Jilly was just a little farther up the road, well within distance for Florian to call out to Caesar without straining. And Finn was there, with Constantine, and would be within distance of the Way as well. Or so they hoped.

"*Are* you going to be all right?" Finn asked, his face anxious and rosy with the cold.

Anthea looked around. They were standing in front of a three-sided shelter that shepherds used in the warmer months. Anthea had a folding cot and blankets, food for herself and the horses, and Finn had started a fire for her in the smoke-blackened corner of the shelter with the peats they had found stacked nearby.

"It's horrifying," she said honestly. "If Miss Miniver, my old schoolmistress, saw me, she would *faint*."

She started to smile, and then it faded.

Anthea was trying very hard not to be jealous of Finn. She waited every day for a letter from the queen, for news, for words of encouragement, for a special mission just for her. She got letters, sporadically, but none containing deep secrets, or orders for her to ride south and rescue anyone. She had argued with Uncle Andrew about taking medicine to Bell Hyde, even though the queen had told her that she and the princesses were well enough and not to come.

So it had been shocking, and more than a little hurtful, that the queen had chosen to tell Finn her secret. The fact that she had authorized Finn to tell Anthea and Jilly, Andrew and Caillin MacRennie only softened it a little. Why did Finn get to be the first one?

According to the queen's official biography, she was from a village called Brambleton, in the northwest, just a few miles

south of Camryn and its fabled castle. She had spent the mod-
est inheritance from her parents' tragic death to go to a Rose
Academy in Blackham, and come to the newly crowned King
Gareth's attention when she had become the youngest Rose
Maiden to his mother, Dowager Queen Louisa.

According to Queen Josephine's letter, she was really from
an obscure village, Upper Stonesraugh, a hidden community
of Leanans south of the Wall. The whole village had taken up
a collection to send her to Blackham, hoping that as a Rose
Maiden she could plead their cause to the outside world.

But things had turned out a bit differently, she had written.
Because she had risen so far, so fast, she had never found any
friends that could be trusted with her secret. In person the
dowager queen, her mother-in-law, was far from the grand-
motherly lady she had seemed to be at official functions. And
the king? All Queen Josephine would say was that she had never
summoned the courage to tell her husband where she was from.

But now the villagers of Upper Stonesraugh had written to
her, begging for help, because the Dag had reached even
their secluded cottages, and they didn't know where else to
turn. They had risked so much in sending her the letter, and
she, in turn, hardly needed to say that she was risking a great
deal in telling Finn her secret.

The most comforting part of the letter had been at the end,
when Queen Josephine assured them that she had already had
ring pox after nursing her oldest daughters through it several

years ago. It was agreed that Finn, Anthea, Jilly, and Caillin MacRennie would take medicine south, with only Finn going to the village itself so that they could conceal their real mission under the guise of making deliveries all along the road.

Finn looked around helplessly. They were knee deep in snow, and the shepherd's hut looked like a strong wind might take the roof right off.

"No, you should come with me," he said. "I can't—this just feels like a bad idea."

"We left Jilly by herself," Anthea pointed out.

"Jilly's . . . *Jilly*," Finn said. "She can take care of herself. I'm mostly worried that she'll shoot anything that moves, and accidentally kill some shepherd looking for a missing lamb or something."

"You don't think I can take care of myself?"

Anthea was offended. She could ride and shoot, had been caring for over a dozen horses on her own the last few weeks, knew how to light a fire and cook over it, and had learned how to administer a vaccine for both horses and humans. When Dr. Rosemary had taught her how to take samples and give inoculations, she had confessed that she hadn't expected the daughter of Genevia Cross to be so . . .

"Intelligent," Dr. Rosemary had finally said, after a long pause. "And yet compassionate."

Anthea had just looked at her, wide-eyed.

"You knew my mother?"

"Unfortunately, yes," Dr. Rosemary had said. "And that is why I was so reluctant to work with you when I first came here. I was in fact shocked that the queen would allow you to be here, knowing who your mother is. But you have proven yourself time and again, and I'm sorry I wasn't more trusting in the beginning."

"Oh, thank you," Anthea had said stiffly, and concentrated on pinching and poking with the needles.

Finn grabbed her gloved hands. "I meant . . . I wish you didn't have to," he said earnestly. "I wish . . . I worry . . . I just . . ."

Now both of their faces were red, but it was not from the cold. Snow was falling thick and fast, coating Finn's blond hair and the shoulders of his gray coat. He needed to leave, or he would be finding his way through the snow to a strange village after the sun set.

Greatly daring, Anthea leaned forward and gave him a quick peck on the cheek, then pulled her hands away.

"Where is your hat?" she said. "And brush the snow off your head before you put it on!"

She fussed around, brushing the snow off Marius and checking the straps that held his supplies in place. Naturally she didn't go near Constantine, who was standing to one side, watching her with suspicion.

"Make sure you stay warm, and keep to the road, and if you can't see the road, promise me you'll stop for the night," she babbled.

"I will, I will," he said, also babbling. "I'm just, oh, here's my hat."

He took a ribbed gray stocking cap out of his coat and pulled it on, after shaking the snow off his hair. Anthea realized that she had knitted that hat; it was the one thing she knew how to knit. She had put it in the warm clothes box in the main hall for anyone who needed it, atop a stack of Jilly's lopsided mittens and Miss Ravel's beautifully cabled scarves. She decided not to say anything about it, since it was already awkward between them, suddenly. But then she caught Finn's eye as she looked away from his hat, and he gave her a slightly crooked smile.

He knew.

"Hurry," she said to him. "And let me know as soon as you get there."

"I will."

He brushed off Con's saddle and swung himself up. Taking the herd stallion, the king of the Leanan horses, out of Leana and into what was essentially enemy territory was a great risk. Finn had done it once before, in order to rescue Anthea, and the weeks that he and Con had spent in Bell Hyde had made everyone at the farm very nervous.

But now, because of the letter from Queen Josephine, he was doing it again. She and Finn were distant cousins, though they still weren't sure how distant or where their families had gotten separated. Finn's family, as far back as anyone knew, had lived north of the Wall since King Kalabar had built it. But, although the queen had been born a magTaran, she was at least the seventh generation of her family raised in Upper Stonesraugh, where Finn was now headed.

Anthea stood in the snow and waved to him until he was out of sight. She knew she didn't need to, she knew it was silly, but she did it anyway. Then she trudged around her small campsite and got ready for the night.

Florian and Leonidas would fit in the shelter, but just barely. She had their saddles off and shoved under the cot, and blankets draped over them. She and Finn had tied their reins inside the shelter, with their rumps sticking out the back, as a temporary solution, but now she did a better job of it. She took their bridles off so that they didn't have to try and eat around the bits, and then, seeing how close they were to the fire, moved everything around again.

She ordered them out for a moment and then pushed the cot across the little room to the fire. Then she brushed the snow off their blankets and brought Florian and Leonidas back inside, so that they were on the opposite side and would have to leap over her and her bed to get to the fire. She took some rope and tied it across the open front of the shelter to make a rough fence, and made herself a pancake for dinner while the horses munched on their feed in the other corner.

Beloved? Florian twisted his neck in the small space and nibbled at the shoulder of her coat. *She Who Is Called Jilly wishes to report for the night. She says that there is nothing left to do but sleep, and so she will sleep.*

Excellent. Tell her I am at a shepherd's hut and Finn has gone on to the village.

She says that she thinks the old tower she is in is haunted, but she is prepared to shoot any ghosts she sees.

Tell Caesar to tell her not to shoot anything unless she is sure it is a dangerous man or a wild animal!

Caesar says that she says that she knew you would say that.

Tell her I mean it.

Anthea settled down to try and sleep. Just as she thought she might actually be drifting off, fully dressed with blankets piled atop her and her beloved coat wrapped tight around her, Florian nudged her with his nose and his mind.

Beloved? I have received word from Constantine.

Yes? Are they all right?

They have reached the village.

And? Did people welcome them? Are they all right?

Anthea sat up on her cot, pulling the blankets to her chin against the cold.

All he has said was that they reached the village.

Anthea was wide awake then. Florian could not get anything else out of Constantine or Marius. She asked Florian to pass the word along to Jilly's horses, but he said that they were all asleep. Was Constantine asleep? Was that why he did not respond? Florian wasn't sure. He reached out to Finn directly, at Anthea's urging, even though it was considered poor manners.

"Manners be hanged," Anthea declared. "You ask Finn if he's all right, right now!"

Florian was quiet for a long time. Anthea stared into the embers of her peat fire and waited.

Beloved?

She put out a hand in the dark and felt Florian's nose.

Yes?

The Now King says that you must wait here. Do not come after him. It will be fine.

Fine? What does that mean?

He is not answering now. That is all he said.

Anthea didn't sleep the rest of the night. Florian and Leonidas, exhausted from their days of travel, let their heads hang and their hips go slack and went to sleep, while Anthea sat up in her blankets, her coat collar around her ears and her back uncomfortably pressed against the rough stone wall of the shelter.

Now that they were there, Anthea had time to think of all the things that might go wrong, if they hadn't already. They had talked at length about what to do if someone shot at them, or tried to destroy the vaccines instead of accepting them. But they hadn't talked about how long to wait for each other, or what to do if the messages passed through the Way seemed too abrupt or vague.

Anthea wished now that they had come up with code words. Certain phrases that meant all was well, or that it was slightly suspicious, or that she should ride back to a place where Florian could reach to the horses at the farm.

She knew they shouldn't need code words, because they had the Way. No one could eavesdrop on them. But still, something seemed off about Finn's reply. If he didn't tell her any more the next day, she fretted over riding after him. That might put her out of range of Jilly's horses. She couldn't help but fear the worst. The horse and human kings of Leana should not have been the ones to go into a strange village, no matter what the queen's message said.

15

THE VILLAGE
IN THE STONES

THE MOMENT ANTHEA WOKE, she and Florian had tried and tried to contact Finn or Marius or even Constantine. For several hours she waited for a response that never came. Sick with worry, she had told Jilly to come quick, but even then could not stand to wait for her.

Anthea didn't bother to pack, and she didn't take Leonidas, which made him huff and pout. She needed to move fast, and Jilly would be there soon enough. Anthea did take her pistol, though, and some water and food for herself and Finn, along with a first aid kit.

What if they had shot Finn?

What if they had thrown his medicine away, and he had done something stupid to try and recover it? The village was full of Leanan families, according to the queen, but they were

Leanans who had never seen a live horse. They had been raised, as Anthea had, as the queen herself had, on the myths of the bad old days when the diseased horses had died and their traitorous riders had been exiled.

"We should have gone with him," Anthea said aloud.

Florian flicked his ears to show that he was listening. He didn't say anything, though, just kept moving ahead, through the trees and snow. They were able to move much faster than Finn, since he'd been leading another horse and both his animals had been heavily laden.

Too heavily laden to run very fast if someone shot at them. Anthea couldn't stop her brain from picturing it. She couldn't think of any other reason why it felt like Finn and his horses were just . . . gone. It wasn't that they hadn't sent her any messages in hours; it was that she couldn't feel them at all. Neither could Florian.

They had disappeared.

The road was easy to distinguish, which was another good thing. Thick brambles grew between the trees, which mostly still had leaves, since this region didn't usually get snow or even very cold temperatures. There were still berries here and there, besides the thorns and random scraps and bits of nature caught in the brambles that made them an impassible wall.

They trotted down the muddy, snowy, awful road with barely any light to guide them. The trees met overhead, and the sky was overcast to boot. Anthea almost broke out into one of Jilly's favorite ballads, just to hear something beyond the pounding of her pulse and Florian's hooves, but didn't dare. She felt like they were already making too much noise.

They broke through the trees and the road ended rather abruptly. Or, it continued on, but the land was so bare that it hardly mattered. The muddy ground ahead of her, patched with snow, showed signs of boot prints, wheels, and the hooves of oxen, but it was all a mess of people heading in different directions.

This didn't alarm her. What did alarm her were the stones. At first Anthea thought they were passing through a gate, but then she looked around and saw that they were actually walking into a ring of standing stones, higher than her head even as she sat on Florian, and as wide as her arms stretched out side to side. They were spaced far enough apart that a pair of carts could have driven through side by side, and the ring stretched away to each side. Anthea couldn't even see the entire ring, because right in the middle was the village.

It was quite large, actually, with a church in the center and a double row of shops and small businesses coming down the main road from the churchyard. The cottages radiated out from the main street in an orderly fashion, and there was one large manor house to the right, which was where Anthea steered Florian. There was no sign of life on the main street, so the manor seemed like the best place to start looking for Finn.

She pointed Florian in that direction, and they passed

between the stones. Anthea brushed at her forehead. It felt like she'd ridden through a cobweb, but there was nothing there. Florian drew up immediately.

What is it, my darling?

Constantine!

But Anthea hardly needed Florian's warning cry. She felt Constantine in her mind abruptly, just as she heard Constantine's scream: the sound of a herd stallion defending his territory, warning the intruders that he was there, and ready to fight.

"That big idiot," Anthea said under her breath. "Is he challenging *us*?"

I shall answer, Florian said.

I suppose you have to. But where is he?

There.

Florian nodded toward the manor house, and then he raised his head and bugled. It wasn't the same challenge that Constantine had issued; Florian would never dare to do such a thing. No, this was merely a response to Constantine, an identification of who Florian was.

"Who does he think it is? What other horses would be here?" Anthea grumbled to herself. *Don't tell him I said that, dear,* she added to Florian.

Anthea gave Florian a gentle nudge with her heels, and he started walking again. After a minute, another call came from Constantine, different from his cry of challenge. Florian speeded up to a trot.

What is it? Where is Finn? Is Marius all right? What did Con say?

The herd stallion bids us come, was Florian's only reply.

As Florian carried her to Constantine, Anthea looked around as best she could. It was a very quaint village. There was no sign of gaslights or motorcars, but everything was neat as a pin and the gray stone and slate roofs of every building made the whole place look carefully planned.

And empty. Where was everyone? Were they all sick in bed? Or . . . dead?

"Finn! Finn!" Anthea yelled his name, but then she felt stupid.

All she was doing was telling whatever villagers were left that there was yet another intruder. She stood up in her stirrups instead and looked around for any sign of life—Finn or a stranger—as Florian continued to follow Constantine's call around a cluster of houses.

Now Anthea saw signs of life, but still no people. There was a cow in the yard behind the first cottage, and chickens. The second had a pair of pigs in a pen well back from the house, which meant that Anthea and Florian passed rather closer to the pigs than Anthea would have liked. But she did notice something.

They've been fed today, she pointed out to Florian. *The cow seemed happy—don't they make a lot of noise when they aren't milked?*

I think so, Florian replied. *Constantine is close!*

They came around another neatly fenced pen—this one with another cow and some chickens—and she could at last see the grounds of the manor house, and the house itself. It was not reassuring. While the other cottages were neatly kept, the gardens cleared for the winter, and the walls and fences in good repair, the manor house had apparently fallen on hard times. Stone walls were tumbling down or smothered under the weight of the garden, which had run wild. Dead grass and flowers clogged the garden, and it took Anthea a moment to realize that most of the wild bushes and climbing plants were roses. Someone had collected the flowers, the hips rather, for teas or whatnot, but hadn't bothered to cut back all the branches that entwined and even choked their way up an ancient, leafless elm tree in the middle of the dead lawn in front of Anthea.

The manor, too, had suffered. The once-rich curtains appeared faded, and though none of the windowpanes were broken, they had the empty-eyed look of a house long-abandoned. It reminded Anthea of the house next door to Uncle Daniel's in Travertine. The family that lived there spent most of their year at their estate in Blackham, and Anthea could always tell whether they were "home" or not.

Florian picked his way along the drive carefully, but stopped halfway to the front door.

"Constantine!" Anthea said aloud. "There you are!"

The herd stallion was in the overgrown garden to the left.

He had his head up and was looking at them. For once he didn't seem to give off waves of hostility, though Anthea was glad she didn't have Arthur with her. Her tiny pet owl always brought out the worst in the massive horse.

Beyond Constantine she saw Marius, who came trotting over to say hello in a much more friendly fashion. Both horses had their tack removed and looked freshly groomed. A net of hay was hanging from a crooked and barren cherry tree to one side as well.

"Where is Finn?" Anthea asked Constantine. *Where is the Now King? Is he safe?*

Constantine had never deigned to acknowledge her before, but she supposed asking about Finn had softened his heart. Or perhaps he was also worried about his king and rider.

Within, go to him.

Constantine's voice was like the scraping of steel on stone in her brain, and she had no sense of his emotions. Was he telling her to go away merely because he didn't like her? Was he telling her to go and help Finn? There was only one way to find out.

She dismounted and unhooked her saddlebags, throwing them over her shoulder. She apologized to Florian for not taking off his saddle and bridle, but she wanted to be ready for a quick escape. She tied his reins in a knot behind his neck so they wouldn't get tangled in his legs, and sent him over the wall. He jumped it neatly and nodded with respect to

Constantine before exchanging a more affectionate greeting with Marius.

Trying to keep her saddlebags on one shoulder and her hand free to draw her pistol at the same time, Anthea walked up the rest of the drive. The big double doors showed the age of the manor: between the iron bands and hinges the wood was dry and the grain stood out in sharp ridges like the lines of an elderly man, only in reverse. One of the double doors was slightly ajar, and Anthea carefully pulled it out just enough that she could slide through. She almost lost her saddlebags in the process, but managed to pull them through without too much noise.

Anthea found herself inside a great hall. There were old banners hanging from the ceiling, and a curving staircase going up ahead of her. It was stone, with well-worn dips in each step and a beautifully carved banister. She hesitated in the middle of the hall. There were doors to the left and right, the stairs, and a smaller door beneath the staircase. Which way had Finn gone? She looked for clues, but could find nothing.

There was no dust. It struck her quite suddenly. There was no dust, no leaves had blown inside, and there was nothing that might show where Finn had gone. The manor was quite clean. There was even, now that her eyes adjusted to the dimness, furniture in the form of small side tables and a long bench. They, too, were free of dust.

"Forget it," Anthea muttered, and then raised her voice. "Finn! Finn? Where are you?"

She heard heavy steps moving quickly toward her from the left. Anthea dropped her saddlebags and unholstered her pistol, her mouth going dry. The door flew open, and someone came barreling toward her.

Anthea screamed and cocked her pistol.

Finn skidded to a stop and threw his hands up in the air. "What are you doing?"

FLORIAN

Beloved Anthea had gone inside the strange house. Florian did not like this. He spoke to Marius and dared to even ask the herd stallion where the Now King was, and if they thought Beloved Anthea and the Now King would be safe.

Constantine would only say that there was much in the village that was strange.

But Marius told Florian much more. They were safe, he assured Florian. All of them. The people did not like the horses, but they had welcomed the medicine that the Now King had brought. They gave him permission to stay in the Big House of this place, and showed him something inside that made him want to stay.

Marius did not know why Florian did not remember this. Marius himself had sent the message shortly after they arrived. Florian hadn't replied to Marius's message, but Marius humbly suggested that perhaps he and his Beloved were simply too caught up in caring for each other.

Florian had not stopped to think of it, but now that he heard the humility and even jealousy in Marius's voice he did, and he was sorry for Marius. Before the Now King had begun to ride the herd stallion, Marius had been his mount. They had been deeply connected, and never had a day passed when the human king-to-be and Marius did not ride out together. But now that the Soon King had become the Now King and taken up his place on Constantine's back, Marius was with him mostly to carry fodder or other supplies.

Marius had not lost any status among the herd; he was still favored by the Now King, but he felt a loss inside. Florian was ashamed to realize he had not thought about Marius's loss of a rider. Perhaps Beloved Anthea should say something to the Now King. Florian could speak to the Now King, but it wouldn't be proper of him, especially since Marius had not done so himself.

Instead Florian asked Marius what he meant that he had sent a message. They had heard nothing. Florian had cried out to Marius and Constantine as well, and gotten no reply, which is why they had come.

Constantine turned to them then.

It is the stones, the herd stallion said. They guard this place. Too well.

16

Uncomfortable Truths

"WHERE HAVE YOU BEEN?" Anthea practically screamed it at Finn.

She shoved her gun into the holster and threw herself at him. She wasn't even embarrassed to hug him tightly and kiss his cheek. Then she pushed herself away just as he tried to hug her back.

Outside, she heard Florian bugling, and hurried to send him a calming thought.

I am all right. Finn startled me. I am all right, and so is he.

"We've been worried sick!" she told Finn.

"What? Why?" He dropped his arms, looking baffled. "I told you that I was looking at these books."

"You did not!"

"Well, I mean, Marius sent a message to Florian, but he was supposed to say the same thing."

"But he didn't! And we tried for hours to reach you, and didn't hear anything!"

"Hours?" Finn blinked hazily at the light coming in through the still open door. "Well, I'm sorry about that. I lost track of time, but I thought you knew we were all right. I told you we got here just fine."

"And then, *nothing*," Anthea pointed out.

"I'm really sorry, I didn't realize!" Finn ran a hand through his blond hair, making it stand on end. "But you have to come and see this!"

He grabbed Anthea's hand without waiting for an answer, and began to drag her toward the room he'd just come from. She reached back for her saddlebags, or to close the door, but he grinned at her and gave another tug on her arm, and she gave in.

Finn brought her into a large room lined with bookshelves. The room was two stories tall and there was a rolling ladder to reach some of the shelves, as well as a spiral staircase leading to a wrought iron catwalk at the far end of the room. Some of the bookshelves had glass doors, and inside them Anthea could see things other than books: astrolabes and barometers, a skull of some animal, stones with markings on them.

There was a fireplace, and some big leather chairs in front of it. But Finn took her to the table he had been using. It was as long as the family dining table at the Last Farm, and of the same massive, heavily carved style. In fact, the mantel and chairs also reminded her of the furnishings at the farm. Much heavier and older looking than anything she had seen in Coronam.

"Leanan," she said softly, putting a finger on the table.

"Exactly!" Finn said in excitement. "And all these!"

Most of the table's surface was covered in books. They were open or had ribbons and rulers and pens and even a spoon sticking out of them to mark places. There was a cup of tea resting on one, and a plate scattered with crumbs on the wooden chair that was pushed back from the table.

"What are they? What do they say?" Anthea asked.

"Everything, Thea," Finn said, clutching her hands. "They say *everything*."

He turned and began to point to random pages in the books, flipping them open and stacking them on top of each other until there was a pile in front of Anthea. She put her hand out to steady it and saw that the book on top was a yellowed report of some kind. She leaned in closer, holding up her free hand to stop Finn from piling on another book.

After the final recurrence left approx. 27 dead, the newly formed parliament judged the disease to be of no further danger. Those who had taken refuge on the north side of King Kalabar's barricade applied to return to the south to reclaim lands forfeited during the height of the outbreaks, but were told there was still a high risk of infection.

Subsequent applications to return to southern
estates or to be compensated for lost property were
met with . . .

"With what?" Anthea said as Finn put another book on top before she could turn the page.

"That?" He lifted the book again and looked at what she'd been reading. "As far as I can tell, there's just one book after another explaining how the Coronami took all the land from the Leanans."

Anthea decided to ignore that. She knew it was true, but it made her feel uncomfortable all the same.

"What's a parliament?" Anthea asked.

"Kronenhof has one," Finn said.

"Oh, right. The people that help . . . make laws?"

"Yes, which apparently we used to have as well. So it wasn't just the king who had power," Finn said. He pulled a couple of books off the pile and set them aside. "See here?" He pointed to a book with very fine print, and then another that was handwritten. "And here." He was moving too fast for Anthea to actually read what he was pointing at, but he didn't seem to care.

"When the Coronami first came, they had a parliament that was half Leanan, half Coronami, so that both people had a say in the governing," Finn said. "But apparently every time a Leanan got sick or died or had to take a leave of absence, they were replaced with a Coronami."

"Who was in charge? Did they have an emperor like Kronenhof?" She frowned. "They had a king," she said, answering herself. "A Leanan king but then—" Her frown deepened.

"The king was gone already," Finn said, shaking his head. He located another book and opened it, but looked at it himself. "He took the herd stallion—or the head herd stallion, rather, because there was more than one herd—and went into hiding."

"He went into hiding?" Anthea couldn't keep the scorn from her voice.

Kings were supposed to be there for their people. They were supposed to lead. The Coronami Crown had always . . .

Anthea let that thought trail away. She knew very well, now, that kings weren't always good and virtuous, and that the Coronami Crown was certainly not the model of all that was noble and good, as she had been taught before going to live at Last Farm. It made sense that maybe, just maybe, some of the Leanan kings hadn't always done the bravest, most noble thing.

Of course, if he had stayed in the south and tried to drive the Coronami out, Finn wouldn't be here.

"Who . . . kept all this?" Anthea asked. "What is this place?"

"We call ourselves the Last *Farm*," Finn said. "And well, this is the Last *Village*. They've been tucked away here for centuries!"

"I know the queen said that in her letter, that they were all Leanan, but . . ." Anthea shook her head in disbelief. "It's so . . . we're so far south! Is the whole village really full of Leanans?"

"Well, the queen is from here, and the queen is Leanan," Finn said. He shrugged.

"A lot of people are part Leanan," Anthea argued. "It makes sense that—"

But now Finn was shaking his head.

"She's full-blooded Leanan, like I am," he said. "In her letter she also told me that I needed to come here myself because I would find things that I needed as much as the people needed medicine."

"What?"

"There was a bit that I was supposed to keep to myself," Finn said, turning red. "That was all of it, though, I swear!"

Anthea fought down another stab of jealousy.

"But how could the king . . . why would he marry someone from an all-Leanan village? He doesn't like us!"

They both stopped for a moment. A year ago, Anthea hadn't even known that she was part Leanan. Eight months ago, she never would have called the Leanans "us." But neither of them commented on this change.

"He didn't know," Finn said. "She said in the letter she could never tell him."

"True, but I still can't believe he didn't . . . doesn't know where his wife is from," Anthea said.

"But it's true, he doesn't," said another voice.

Anthea spun around, hand to her pistol again. She relaxed slightly when she saw that it was an elderly man in a tweed jacket, smiling kindly at her from the doorway of the library. His white hair was curly and his blue eyes twinkled.

"Are you . . . ? Do you know . . . ?" She stammered.

"Oh, aye," he said, coming into the room. "I'm Josephine's uncle."

Anthea sent a quick message to Florian to stand down. Her constant jumping and grabbing at her gun had put him on edge, and he was currently hovering near the corner of the wall that was closest to the house. She was worried that he would jump the wall and come barging into the house itself.

I have just met the uncle of Josephine, Beloved of Holly, Anthea told him.

A good uncle or a bad uncle? Florian fretted. His experience with her uncle Daniel had taught him to be cautious of uncles.

He has her kind eyes! she assured him.

That seemed to settle Florian, and then she realized that the queen's uncle was watching her patiently. When her gaze focused on him again, he nodded.

"Talking to your horses?"

"Just . . . just the one," she said.

"You're the full-blooded Leanan girl," he said. "The one who rides stallions?"

"I'm not full-blooded . . . but yes, I have a stallion," Anthea said uncertainly. "His name is Florian."

It was a good thing that Leonidas couldn't hear her. She was sure he would be offended to think that he didn't count as one of "her" stallions. But still, despite his kind eyes, she didn't think this man needed to know all the details about her and her horses, queen's uncle or not. After all, she didn't even know his name.

"I'm the MagTaran," the man said.

"The . . . MagTaran?"

Finn's last name was magTaran, and so was the queen's. Anthea was confused.

"So, is everyone in this village a magTaran?" she asked.

"Many of them are," the MagTaran said. "My mother was, and I am actually a MacRennie."

"Like Caillin MacRennie," Finn said, nudging Anthea as though she could have missed that connection.

But Anthea was just blinking at the old man. "So, wait, you're . . ."

"The MagTaran is a title," the man explained. "Rather like a lord mayor. The magTaran family founded the village, and I'm the oldest member of the family, so I'm *the* MagTaran."

"I just . . . there's so much I don't understand," Anthea said helplessly.

She sank back on the chair behind her, and a book fell off onto the floor. She looked down at it. It was a collection of Leanan ballads.

"Jilly would love that," Anthea said, almost absently.

"She is welcome to come and look at it," the MagTaran

said, sitting across the table from her. "But it cannot leave this house. Part of my job is to collect, and protect, the knowledge of our people. This is all that is left, of our entire nation." He gestured around the library.

"But how could you all be here for so long, and—" Anthea began.

She didn't know how to end that sentence, though. How could they be here for so long without everyone marrying their cousins, which she knew from Miss Miniver was not a good idea? How could they be here for so long without everyone knowing they were here? Without King Gareth knowing where his own wife was from?

Once again, The MagTaran seemed to know exactly what she was thinking. Afterward she would begin to wonder, uneasily, if he had the Way, but with people.

"We have sent many of our people out, over the years," he said sadly. "We had to. For work. For marriage. Sometimes they found husbands and wives who wanted to come back with them. Sometimes they did not." He sighed heavily. "And sometimes we told them never to come back."

"You mean, they had to be exiled?"

"For the good of the people, yes," he said, looking at her squarely. "Like my niece. My Josie."

"What?"

"We sent her away," the MagTaran said. "On purpose. We wanted to have a Rose Maiden, someone placed near the Crown, who could perhaps whisper in the royal ears and tell them of our village. Smooth the way for us to come out of the shadows. Find out if the rumors about horses surviving were true."

"The queen was sent away when she was even younger than we are," Finn burst out, unable to contain the things he had learned any longer. Anthea couldn't blame him.

"We knew she could make it into the inner circles of the old queen," the MagTaran said. "We just never expected she would rise so high." He still sounded sad.

"Aren't you pleased for her? Or proud of her?" Anthea asked.

"Of course! Of course I am," he said. "But you realize that she has never been able to come back? The king himself, her own husband, thinks she's from Brambleton."

"But she *told* me she was from a tiny village when I first met her," Anthea protested. "Oh. *Oh.*"

The queen had never said the *name* of the village. The queen had never lied; she just hadn't told the whole truth.

"Her own husband doesn't know?" Anthea almost whispered it.

The MagTaran shook his head. Anthea felt her eyes prickle. How lonely that must be! She had often wondered about the queen. She was such a bright, happy person, with her Rose Maidens and her four daughters gathered around her always. But so often now she was at Bell Hyde, away from Travertine. And the king.

"Poor Josephine," Anthea murmured. "I mean, Her

Majesty," she said, seeing their eyes on her. "No," she said, shaking her head. "*Josephine*. Poor Josephine." She blinked her eyes rapidly.

"Precisely," the queen's uncle said warmly. "We thought, as a mere Rose Maiden, perhaps the wife of someone highly placed, she might be able to open up channels between us and the rest of Coronam. But her life became even more restricted." His smile broadened. "Until you and your cousin showed up on her doorstep with a herd of horses."

"The king was so angry," Anthea whispered.

"But not at Josephine," the MagTaran assured her. "If he finds out the secrets she has kept, like this house and its library, he will be angry at her. And that is not good for a woman in her position." His face tightened as he said it, and the corners of his mouth turned down.

"What do you mean? What position?" Anthea looked from him to Finn.

"They have four daughters," Finn reminded her. "And no son."

"But he can't do anything about that," Anthea said. "And neither can she."

"He can put her aside and take a new queen," The Mag-Taran said. "And there has apparently been some talk of that, according to one of our people."

"He would never do that!" Anthea gasped.

Putting aside a spouse was almost unheard-of in Coronam.

Anthea had heard of women leaving their husbands because they committed some terrible crime, but to get rid of your wife just because you wanted a son? Surely that couldn't happen . . . not to a queen! The scandal would be far too great.

"Who could have told you this, though?" Finn said. "I thought you had almost no contact with the outside?"

"That is true, we mostly do what little outside dealings with have with the nearby villages," the MagTaran said. "Post comes once a month, which is about how often any of us leaves to go to market."

Anthea relaxed. They were far from the reaches of actual court news. This was surely just nervous speculation on the MagTaran's part.

"But we do have a spy," he went on. "And she does not think Josie will still be queen next year."

17

THE LAST MANOR

ANTHEA WALKED SLOWLY THROUGH the manor. It was a strange place. It reminded her very much of the Big House at Last Farm. Although it was several stories tall, there was a low, wide quality to all the rooms and corridors, different from the high but narrow look of most Coronami houses. It wasn't oppressive, though, and the windows were all wide, with clear panes that let in plenty of light, and plenty of lamps.

But the manor had an odd feel because it was somewhere between a house and a museum. Some rooms, like the library, were set up to be used, but others were crammed with things that had been arranged as best they could in the limited space. The sitting room, for instance, had four long sofas wedged into it, among the small tables and high-backed chairs, and none of them matched. There were knickknacks on every surface, too:

balls carved of solid wood or stone, some of them painted with scenes of gardens or fields, sitting in low wooden holders to keep them from rolling away. There were horseshoes that had been gilded or painted or were carved of wood, and garlands made of intricately braided hair from horses' tails draped across mantels.

"We thought the horses were dead," the MagTaran said, strolling along behind her. "When Josie got me the message, a few months ago, I couldn't believe it. All my life, all my father's and grandfather's lives, we collected whatever artifacts we could."

He waved a hand at the walls of the corridor they were walking down. Portraits were hung from the ceiling down to the floor, a mixture of styles, the frames practically touching, and none of the people looking remotely related. There were little plaques on the frames with the name of the sitter and the artist, though many of them were blank or had a question mark after the name.

"But we thought we'd never see a horse in the flesh. Many of our people were starting to think they never existed at all, that they were fabulous creatures like dragons. Or that we once worshipped them, instead of working with them."

"I would think more people would come to see them, then," Anthea said. She had had no message from Florian that he had seen another person, and there was no challenge from Constantine.

"Too many are ill," the MagTaran said heavily. "The rest are ordered to stay at home at all costs. I have distributed the medicine, and the instructions for inoculating and taking samples, but . . ." He sighed. "It is so strange. We had heard only the vaguest rumors of illness, keeping to ourselves as we are. There have been only a handful of sick in the nearby villages, but still we cut off contact with them.

"And then suddenly one day, a dozen were sick."

They stopped and peered into one of the bedrooms. It was the one Finn had slept in, the bed was a mess, his saddlebags were on the floor, and Anthea blushed to see some anonymous bit of boy underclothing straggling across the floor. There were three washbasins in the room, she noticed when she quickly raised her eyes, and four water pitchers. They moved along.

"You can stay here," the MagTaran told her.

They opened the door to another bedroom. This one had a long, low padded bench running along the end of the bed, and two huge upholstered chairs crowded against the window. The bed was also enormous, bare except for the mattress, and there was a large chest between it and the far wall.

"The linens are in that chest," the MagTaran said. "It might be a bit tricky getting the lid up to reach them," he added ruefully.

"Thank you, but I think first I had better ride out of the village and see if my Florian can't get a message to my cousin and her horses," Anthea said, her eyes longingly on the bed.

The mattress was very thick, and there was an enormous pile of pillows.

"That is so strange," the MagTaran said. "We never knew the stones were anything special. Of course, we never knew if the Way was real or not, either, until Josie. And now Prince Finn, and you."

It was odd to hear Finn called a prince. In the back of her head, Anthea was always aware that he was a king, but no one ever addressed him as such. At least, no humans did. But something else bothered her more.

"So Josie—Queen Josephine—has never come here with her horses?"

"Oh, naturally not," the MagTaran said. "She hasn't been back since she left us as a wee girl! Even getting a letter here directly is difficult. She has to send it through a network of those who have moved out of the village. Some of them keep in touch with family, and will pass on a letter that cannot be sent through the post."

"Do a lot of people who leave come back?" Anthea asked. "I mean, to stay?"

They were continuing down the corridor and he was showing her other bedrooms. They were all tidy, and unlived in. Someone obviously dusted and swept regularly, though the MagTaran insisted that no one lived here.

"It's rare," he said sadly. "One of the few who has ever come back is our great lady," he said, pointing to a room at the end of the corridor. "She's the one who has brought many of the things here, especially the books."

"Your . . . great lady?"

Something cold slithered down Anthea's spine.

"Her mother left, very young. She had wandering ways," the MagTaran said with faint distaste. "When her daughter came back to us, a fine lady, highly placed among the Coronami, well, we were very shocked. But also very grateful. She always brings us lost things: books, paintings, bits of information." He gestured around the hallway. "The collection in the manor has doubled, if not tripled, thanks to her."

"Did she know about Last Farm?" Anthea kept her voice carefully neutral.

"She would have told us if she had," the MagTaran said. "I cannot wait for her to return; she will be so delighted! She has traveled a great deal, but never beyond the Wall. A woman in her position cannot, you know. Not without the proper reasons, or a chaperone." He shook his head at Anthea as though she should know this.

Anthea put one hand on the doorknob of the room. The MagTaran sucked in a breath.

"That's the lady's room," he chided her. "It would be rude to disturb it."

"I—I think I—I have to see," Anthea stammered. "I think . . . I know her?"

Anthea's heart was hammering. She was praying rapidly

and silently that she didn't know their great lady. She twisted the doorknob. It was locked.

"Only the lady has a key," the MagTaran said. "And it's quite impossible that you would know her: as I said, she has never been north of the Wall."

"Oh, of course," Anthea said. She turned away, putting her hands in the pockets of her coat. "I'm very sorry.

"But would you tell me: What is her name?"

"Lady Vivian," he said at once, in reverent tones.

Anthea's racing heart began to slow. The cold sweat stopped trickling down her back.

"Ah," Anthea said. "You're right. I don't know her."

"She could return at any time," the MagTaran assured her. "I would like you to meet her. And I know she will be thrilled to meet you and your horses!"

Anthea followed him downstairs again, declining his offers to wash, to rest, to have help getting her room ready. She waved a hand through the door at Finn, but wasn't sure he saw, he was so intent on the book he was reading.

"I must tell my cousin what's happening," Anthea said. "I'll be back as soon as I can."

She hurried down to the enclosure and climbed the wall. Florian came to meet her, and she stood atop the wall to more easily slide onto his back.

Beloved?

Something is wrong, my love, Anthea told him.

The Woman Who Smells of Dying Roses?

That was Florian's name for her mother. He could see it in her mind, her fear that it was her mother whose room was at the end of the corridor. But Lady Vivian? And why would her mother gather these things, the Leanan books and furniture, and bring them to a safe place? No, it was irrational. This couldn't be her mother.

But something was just wrong all the same.

Let's go talk to Jilly, she told Florian. *Or rather, let's go talk to Caesar.*

This time, passing through the village, they saw signs of life. People were coming out of their cottages to feed animals and do a few chores. They stopped to watch Anthea go by, and she raised a hand to them. She didn't see any children, and the people she did see were thin and worn looking, even from a distance. They had clearly been ill, and she hoped that the vaccine had come in time.

Up on the hill, Anthea felt a ripple as she passed between the standing stones. There was definitely something about them. She pulled Florian to a halt as soon as they were through, and told him to send a message to Jilly via Caesar.

We're already on our way to you, the reply came. *All of us.*

It seemed that Jilly had panicked when Anthea had suddenly gone silent, and Caesar could not get a response from Florian. She had gathered all the horses, sent a message to Caillin MacRennie, and was cautiously on her way to the village, trying to stay alert for ambush, and probably with her pistol cocked, Anthea thought with a sigh.

Tell Jilly not to shoot anyone, and to go straight to the manor, Anthea said.

She decided to head back and get something to eat with Finn, rather than wait in the cold for Jilly and the other horses. And speaking to Jilly had given her an idea about that locked room.

When Anthea had first arrived at Last Farm, she had decided to try and teach her cousin to be a proper young lady, to train her the way Anthea had been trained as a Rose Candidate. Some of this behavior had rubbed off on Jilly, it was true, but it was mostly by accident. But Anthea had learned far more from Jilly than Jilly had from her. Miss Miniver, Anthea's former headmistress, would probably approve of some of these things, like the proper way to apply cosmetics, but would definitely not approve of some of them, like how to alter men's trousers to fit a young lady.

And how to pick locks.

Anthea had tea with Finn and the MagTaran in the library. While they ate, Finn showed Anthea more things that he had found, and the MagTaran filled them in on other bits of the history of the village. Apparently standing stones had been common around lords' houses and their attendant villages, but most of the others had been pulled down and the stones used for new houses and churches by the Coronami.

"But what kind of stone is it?" Anthea asked. "It's very slick and solid looking."

"It's stone," Finn said. He laughed, but not unkindly.

Anthea flushed all the same. "Oh, you know what I mean," she said, resisting the urge to throw a biscuit at him as she would have at home. "You can't see any little . . . grains . . . or bits of different rocks in there. I noticed it coming back just now. It almost looks like steel."

"We don't know where it was quarried," the MagTaran said. "We don't even know if the other estates had rings made of the same stones. None of the houses here are made of it. It never chips or shows much wear, even after all these years. I can't imagine that they could have used the same stone to build houses."

"So perhaps the other estates didn't block the Way?" Finn said thoughtfully. "But if it was just this one, I wonder if some property of the stone also kept you from being discovered." He began to flip through a book at his elbow.

"Over here, I think," the MagTaran said, and reached an old book off the shelf next to the fireplace.

"I'm just going to go freshen up," Anthea said, standing.

Finn and the MagTaran barely spared her a glance. Anthea didn't waste time being offended. She hurried out of the library and up the worn stairs. She opened and closed the door of the room she had been assigned, loudly, without going in, and then tiptoed on down the passage to the locked room at the end.

Jilly kept her lock-picking tools stuck inside hats or used them as hairpins, but pins always slithered out of Anthea's hair and she didn't like hats. Instead she kept them in a thin leather wallet she always had in a pocket, along with a small photograph of her father Uncle Andrew had given her.

She slipped the metal picks out, taking just a moment to look at the picture of her father. He would have been beside himself with joy, as Finn was, to find an entire village of Lean-ans. The moment they were well enough, he would be running them all through the manor garden to see if they had the Way. She had no doubt that Uncle Andrew would soon be on his way here, to do the same.

But first she had to find out if her suspicions were true. She had been relieved to hear that the MagTaran's "great lady" was named Vivian. But at the same time . . . the queen herself did not dare to come and go from this village. So who was this Lady Vivian who was so free about it?

Anthea slipped the first pick into the lock and felt for it to catch. Then the next, then she twisted. The door swung open, creaking a little, and Anthea froze. When there was no sound from downstairs she tucked her picks away and slipped into the room.

It was beautifully furnished and felt lived in, unlike the rest of the house. But there was nothing that Anthea could see that marked it as particularly distinct. The paintings, the linens, the furniture, were all the same as the rest of the house, though better arranged and not half as cramped. The desk was clear of any papers, the only book a Kronenhofer novel that had been all the rage two years ago.

Anthea went to the dressing table. There was face powder, but nothing fancy, and a crystal bottle of perfume with a gold stopper. Anthea picked it up to sniff it.

It smelled like roses. It was the signature scent of Rose Maidens and Matrons. Anthea put it down so fast that she almost tipped it over and only caught it at the last second. The stopper flew out and rolled across the table, falling to the floor with a small chime.

Anthea knelt down, the scent of the rose perfume filling her nostrils and making her feel strange. It reminded her both of her mother and Queen Josephine, and brought a sudden sting of tears to her eyes. She groped under the table and found the stopper, causing something else to roll away. She picked them both up and put the stopper in the bottle before getting stiffly to her feet, still sore from her uncomfortable night in the hut.

She looked down at her hand. She was holding a narrow glass tube, exactly like the ones favored by Dr. Rosemary for her samples. This one was empty, and a bit dusty on the outside, with a dried streak of something yellow in the bottom.

Anthea's heart shot into her throat. She dropped the tube, not caring when it broke on the tabletop, and began scrubbing her hand against her trousers as she backed away. Something touched her shoulder, and she spun around and let out a little scream, thinking there was someone in the room with her, but it was a wooden bust with a hat on it on a table by the wardrobe. Anthea's heart didn't stop racing, though. Instead it speeded up.

The hat was as large as a cartwheel, with cream-colored veils draped artfully around it. And beneath the veiling the brim of the hat was thickly decorated with dozens of red silk roses.

Anthea knew that hat. She would never forget the first time she had seen that hat, terrified and wounded as she had been at the time.

Anthea slammed the door shut behind her and ran down the stairs, not even caring about the clatter she made. In the library, Finn and the MagTaran looked at her strangely when she came racketing in, panting and clutching her side as though to protect the long-healed wound.

"We have to go," she said to Finn. "*Right now.* We have to get out of here."

"What? What are you talking about?"

"Is it the horses?" the MagTaran asked with concern. "Did something happen to them?"

Anthea looked at Finn, trying to convey that she needed to speak to him privately, but he just blinked at her while the MagTaran asked again what was wrong.

"Lady Vivian is a *lie*," Anthea announced. "Their great benefactress is my *mother*!"

18

FLEEING

"I'M NOT STAYING HERE," Anthea said.

Her voice was shaking and she didn't care. Florian butted her with his nose and she took hold of his mane for comfort.

"I won't stay here. None of us should," she said in a clearer voice.

They were standing in the front garden of the manor, a cluster of riders and horses. Jilly and Caillin MacRennie had arrived just in time to hear the horrified Anthea pleading with Finn to saddle up Constantine and leave with her.

"I'm with Anthea," Jilly said. "We are not staying here to let her mother the spy wander up and shoot us all."

"Anthea's mother isn't the one who shot her," Finn said reasonably.

Anthea nearly snatched off his hat—the one she had

knitted! How dare he stand there wearing a hat she had knitted and act so superior? He didn't know her mother!

Of course, she herself barely knew her mother, a little niggling voice cut into her brain. And there were no witnesses. She might have been overreacting. She had been feverish, injured, tired. But she would never forget her mother's voice calmly discussing getting rid of all the horses but Florian. That had been no fever dream. And then there was what else Dr. Rosemary had told Anthea, when she had said that she knew Genevia Cross-Thornley.

"Before my mother broke with the queen completely," Anthea said icily, "she toured the scientific college where Dr. Rosemary and her colleagues were just beginning their studies. A week later, the king tried to shut them down, saying that they were building bombs and fomenting treason. It was all Queen Josephine could do to convince her husband that they were innocent."

"Well," Finn said uneasily. "I just—"

"And," Anthea said, and was surprised at the catch in her voice, the prickle in her nose. "And when I went to Parsiny with that little boy, Tim? His grandfather . . . his grandfather told me that my mother had gotten him exiled. And I think that someone else was executed because of her."

"Oh, no," Jilly whispered. She put a hand on Anthea's arm. "Is that why you were so upset when you came back?"

Anthea could only nod. Jilly leaned closer and stroked her

hair. Anthea could still hear Tim's chipper little voice in her head, saying that the men had found books in Camryn that the king didn't like. Camryn, just up the road from Upper Stonesraugh. Had Genevia stopped there to tour the castle on one of her wonderful trips to her home village? And what was it that Sir Timothy and his friend had confided to her, this beautiful Rose Maiden who had gotten one of them killed and the other exiled?

"And now," Anthea plowed on, forcing her voice to be steady, "I found a tube of something nasty in her room. She opened a sample of the Dag here, she made these people sick somehow! I know she did!"

"Finn, lad," Caillin MacRennie said. "It's a terrible enough thing to bring the herd stallion this far south. Whether or not it's Anthea's mother who is their great benefactress, the medicine's been delivered, and we should get Con back to the farm."

"But these books, Caillin MacRennie!" Finn sounded desperate. "We have to study them!"

"We also need to test these folks for the Way," Caillin MacRennie agreed. "And collect the samples that Dr. Rosemary has her heart set on.

"But I won't stand for having that awful—I mean, well, Anthea's mother," he amended hastily. "I won't stand for having her and the herd stallion in the same country!"

"Didn't she use to live at the farm?"

Anthea asked the question before she could stop herself. She wanted to get them out of there, not drag on the conversation.

But she couldn't resist asking. She knew so little about either of her parents. And how they had ended up together.

"Aye," Caillin MacRennie said. "Off and on. Played it like she was just a blushing bride, frightened o' the horses, without a friend or relation in the world, doing the bidding of her dear, dear queen."

"Without a relation?" Jilly gave Anthea a puzzled look. "Don't you have roughly a thousand aunts and uncles?"

"Uncle Daniel and Aunt Anne are my mother's half brother and sister," Anthea clarified. "And they made sure that I knew they were only *half.* Their father had been married before, and she died after having my mother, and then he married their mother. And there are a lot of great-aunts and -uncles, and cousins twice removed," Anthea said. "They were the ones passing me around all those years. Some of them aren't really related to me, which they also made sure I knew." She couldn't keep the bitterness out of her voice, but when Jilly started to say something supportive, Anthea held up a hand.

"Vivian," she said. "My mother's mother's name was Vivian." She closed her eyes for a moment. "We *have* to leave," she said.

"Are you sure you're not grasping at straws?" Finn demanded.

"Why would I want this to be true?" Anthea said hotly, opening her eyes to glare at him. "You think that I don't want to read all these books, too? But I know that's her hat. I know that's her perfume—"

"All Rose Maidens wear that perfume," Finn argued. "Or

so you've told me. And a lot of them wear hats and things with roses on them."

"Even *Florian* knows that hat," Anthea insisted. "And the fact that they didn't have the illness until a few weeks ago—I think she brought it here on purpose!"

"I still don't understand," Jilly wailed. "*When* did Anthea's mother turn evil? I mean, yes, the train, horrible," she said, seeing Anthea's face. "But they love her here, don't they?" Jilly clutched at her curls. "What is happening?"

"She always was horrifying," Caillin MacRennie said. "She was just very good at hiding it. Always off on a shopping spree in the south, or going to wait upon the queen, even though she was just the lowliest of lowly Rose Matrons, or so she said." He was shaking his head. "Charles wasn't a fool. He put it all together. Some big to-do with the Kronenhofer ambassador, or the Kadiji princes, was always happening right when she got a hankering to buy some new gowns." He rubbed a rough hand over his face. "People *died* when Genevia Cross-Thornley was around. Important people. Deals were made, governments made deals that benefitted the Coronami and not their own people. And then she'd come sailing back, shopping bags in tow and butter not melting in her mouth.

"Charles just loved her too much to see it."

"But she never told Gareth about the horses," Finn said, sounding hopeful.

"That I can't reckon," Caillin MacRennie said. "Either she

did love Charles, or she was waiting to use the horses as bait in her plot when the time was right."

"She also never told this village that horses still survived," Anthea countered.

"So is she working for herself now?" Jilly said. "I thought King Gareth hated her. For not telling him about Last Farm."

"I don't know," Anthea said. "I wish I did—no, that's not true. I wish I'd never met her. I wish I'd been born in a stable, and didn't have a mother!"

They all looked at her, Finn and Caillin MacRennie uncomfortable, Jilly sympathetic. She patted Anthea's shoulder.

"Mothers are horrible," she said with feeling.

"The MagTaran won't let these books out of his sight," Finn said, changing the subject. "And I *need* to read them!"

"Fine," Anthea said shrilly, throwing her hands up. "Stay! But I am taking Florian and Leonidas, and I am leaving this place!"

Anthea had both her horses ready to go. She wanted Finn to come with her, to tell the queen in person about everything they had discovered and what they suspected about the Dag, but if he wouldn't come, then she and Jilly would go on their own. She mounted Florian and turned him around, taking up Leonidas's lead. Jilly was on Caesar in an instant, with Buttercup at her heel. They looked at Finn, at his desperate face.

"I have to stay," he said. "I'm trying to help all of us."

"Very well, lad, very well," Caillin MacRennie said. He

paused. "I can't stay, because Mistress Cross-Thornley knows me all too well. Are you all right on your own?"

"Of course!"

Finn's face was alight, and Anthea tried not to feel too angry about it. They really could use the information Finn found here.

"Do you think you can send Con with me?" Caillin Mac-Rennie said doubtfully.

They all paused.

"Er, no, I'd better not," Finn said. "I don't think he would like that at all."

Caillin MacRennie sighed. "Aye, probably not. But you'd best find a better, more discreet place for him," he admonished Finn. "Come back to the farm as soon as you can. And test the villagers for the Way."

"I will," Finn said. He lowered his voice. "I'll see if I can't convince the MagTaran to let me take some of the books to show Andrew."

"This is a terrible idea," Jilly announced.

Anthea didn't bother to reply. She was hurt by Finn's refusal to listen to her, and very, very scared. Lady Vivian, Genevia Cross-Thornley, her mother, was dangerous. Anthea knew this deep in her bones. She couldn't begin to understand what her mother had done, let alone why. Leaving Finn here, with the herd stallion, was a terrible idea.

They crossed out of the standing stones, and Anthea felt a sudden blankness in her mind. It was a relief to no longer be able to feel Constantine's tangle of emotions, rage always at the forefront. He was so angry all the time, and Anthea could not understand it. He was a king, his every whim catered to . . . it was just never enough for the big stallion.

❧

The next day, Anthea and Jilly left Caillin MacRennie at the abandoned tower where Jilly had been waiting before. It was getting dark already, but they pressed on, wanting to go as far as they could before they needed to stop.

"It's nice to be able to use the main road, like a decent human being," Jilly offered after they had been riding in silence for an hour.

"Why is Con always so angry?"

"What? Is he?" Jilly looked at Anthea in astonishment.

"His emotions are like pushing your face into a blackberry bramble," Anthea said. She felt like her analogy was a stroke of genius, and resolved to write it down later.

"But I *like* blackberries," Jilly retorted.

Anthea opened her mouth, but Jilly cut her off.

"I'm not saying it's a bad thing, and I'm not saying I'm as jealous as I used to be," Jilly said very seriously. "But you have to understand: I don't have the Way the way you have the Way. No one has the Way as you have the Way." She laughed a little at what she was saying, but she sobered quickly. "Anthea!" She pulled up Caesar and swung her leg across the saddle so that she could look directly at her cousin. "You're Leanan!"

"Um, yes? As are you," Anthea said, confused.

"No! Don't you see! It's no wonder your gift is so strong! Your father was Leanan, and your mother is, too!"

Anthea slumped on Florian's back like a sack of potatoes. If her mother was really from Upper Stonesraugh, not Bellair . . . and her father was from Leana and the Last Farm . . . *Beloved?*

"But . . . but she lied," Anthea said, to Jilly and Florian. And Leonidas and Caesar and Buttercup, who were listening and pretending not to. "I mean, she always lies! It's just . . . lies," Anthea repeated uncertainly.

"I don't think it is, for once," Jilly said. "Think about it: I'm only half Leanan, and my father is actually only half Leanan. Did you know?"

Anthea shook her head. She hadn't known.

"That's how we got a name like Thornley," Jilly said. She switched her leg over and they started riding again. "Dashton Thornley, our great-grandfather, was an exile." She waggled her eyebrows at Anthea. "A smuggler, a pirate, and a loudmouth who had a lot to say to the old king, Frederick, which Frederick did not care for. He ended up at Last Farm, with his wife and their son, who fell in love with both horses and Alisa MacRennie—she was Caillin MacRennie's aunt. So we are related, but not that closely." Jilly flapped a hand, cutting off Anthea before Anthea could ask.

"I never knew," Anthea said, but quietly, because Jilly was still on a roll and Anthea wanted to hear all this.

"Yes, yes, it's actually very convoluted and Caillin MacRennie's first wife died and his second wife ran away with a blacksmith, so the only thing he likes to talk about are horses," Jilly warned. "So Grandfather Thornley married a nice local girl with the Way, had your father and mine, they both died rather young, in a sailing accident. From what I can tell, our family has been one Leanan marrying one Coronami for years."

Anthea wasn't quite sure that was true. What about Grandmother Thornley? She was "local" did that mean an exile or a native Leanan? It made her head ache.

"Then my father married my mother, who was certainly Coronami," Jilly went on bitterly. "After meeting her on a walking holiday . . . something which I still do not understand." Jilly shook her head and patted her mount's neck. "Walking," she muttered.

"But *your* father," she said, turning to Anthea. "Your father married a Leanan, he just didn't know it!"

"Someone has to have known it," Anthea said. "Assuming that my mother was telling the truth when she said that her mother was from Upper Stonesraugh. That means that she is only half Leanan, and I still don't understand how my mother and father ended up getting married."

"Well," Jilly said slowly. "I've never done it myself, but I think you need a church, a priest, a—"

Anthea snapped the end of her reins at her cousin's leg.

"Ouch!"

"I mean," Anthea said ominously. "I have heard all my life

how the queen arranged my parents' marriage. I thought it was because my mother was her favorite Rose Maiden. Josie—Queen Josephine—"

"Let's call her Josie," Jilly interjected. "I love that name!"

"Josie, then, implied that she did it because she was trying to keep my mother on her side." Anthea frowned. "But if she didn't know about the horses, and she did know that my mother was on the verge of betraying her to become the king's personal spy—" Anthea's temples throbbed.

"You know what I like about you, Thea?" Jilly's tone was breezy.

"We're cousins? Sometimes I let you dress me?"

"I like the way you no longer run and hide in your room when we talk about your mother," Jilly said. "It's so much easier to have a conversation with you when you're not having the vapors every five minutes!"

Snap.

"Ouch! You brat!"

"Don't call me a brat, I'll go to my room and hide," Anthea mock-threatened.

"Well!" Jilly huffed. "The good news is, we are on our way to the queen. And when we get there, we can just ask Josie herself about your mother!"

Anthea wondered if it was too late to have the vapors after all.

CONSTANTINE

The human fillies were gone, and this was good. They had taken Florian and Leonidas, who said that they would not challenge Constantine to be herd stallion, but he did not like them all the same. Florian, in particular, was troublesome.

But not as troublesome as the human filly that Florian loved so much. That Anthea. The Now King should not be listening to her. It was not the right of mares and fillies to tell the herd stallion what to do, nor his rider.

Constantine did not like this place. He did not like the ring of stones that kept him from connecting to his herd. He did not like that That Anthea was right and his rider was wrong: they should have left. They should have all left, and returned to their home in the north.

This place did not smell right.

19

TURN AROUND

THEY WERE A DAY away from Bell Hyde when they saw something heading toward them. Anthea wasn't sure what it was at first. This far to the south there was no snow, so the weather was cold but dry, and whatever it was had a plume of dust behind it.

Anthea drew up, guiding her horses to the side of the road. Jilly followed, remarking that it was the first motorcar they had seen all day.

"Which is both good and bad, I suppose," she said. "I mean, I hope there aren't so many people . . . well, dead, from the Dag. But it's nice to not worry about being threat—That's a *horse*!"

It was indeed a horse, coming fast up the road. The rider was small, clinging to the back of a bay mare with tall white stockings.

"That's Blossom!"

Anthea and Jilly shouted it together, and then they moved back to the center of the road to intercept the rider. Blossom slowed immediately, but they could see the rider urging her faster, so focused that she didn't even seen Florian and Caesar blocking the way. Anthea dropped the reins to wave her arms, and Florian neighed.

Blossom skidded to a stop just in time.

"Hey!" The rider raised her head. She had a dark green scarf tied around her hair, but a few gold curls were escaping.

"Princess Margaret!"

Anthea stared at the princess in shock. The princess blinked back at them, equally stunned. Jilly came to her senses first.

"Walk her, walk!" she ordered.

Blossom was lathered and blowing hard. Anthea had no idea how long she had been running, but she was instantly glad that they had caught her before Blossom was injured.

"Walk, walk," Anthea said, taking up the chant. *Walk, Blossom dear!* she said as reinforcement.

Florian and Caesar fell in on each side of Blossom, and they began to walk back the way they had come, in the direction the princess had been going. The other horses meekly followed, and Anthea felt their waves of concern for Blossom. She was a good horse for running so hard when she was asked to, and the princess didn't know any better, Anthea whispered to the mare through the Way.

How are you? Are you teaching Princess Margaret how to be a rider?

Yes. She has become dear to me, Blossom replied. *I only wanted to do as she asked. Our message is most urgent.*

What is it?

Anthea repeated the question aloud. "What is your message? Where were you going?"

"To find you," Princess Margaret said.

"We're on our way to bring you the vaccine, Your Highness," Anthea told her. They kept walking back up the road, however. Part of Anthea's mind was still concerned with Blossom's breathing.

"We've all had ring pox," the princess said. "And please, call me Meg," she added, almost shyly.

Jilly's face lit up. "We're Jilly and Thea," she said eagerly. "Not Jillian and Anthea, and this is going to be so fun!"

"Thank you, Your . . . Meg," Anthea said.

She was very pleased and flattered to be asked to call a royal princess by her nickname. But she was also very worried about why the queen had sent her youngest daughter, alone, on a horse, to find them.

"Why did you need to find us so urgently?" Anthea asked.

"It's your mother, Anthea. Thea," Meg said. "She . . . I'm sorry, do we need to keep riding? I feel like, like I need to be on the ground or something before I say this."

Anthea and Jilly exchanged looks, then they steered the

horses over to the side of the road. Anthea tied up the horses while Jilly showed Meg how to rub down Blossom's legs to keep them from cramping.

Anthea tied the reins so tight that she got her finger caught and broke one of her already too short nails. Her mother. Again.

"Blossom wants a drink," Meg said.

"In a minute," Jilly said. "Horses sometimes want things that aren't good for them, when they've been running hard or are hurt."

Jilly was getting the water skins from the packhorses, but Anthea couldn't wait any longer. Neither could Meg.

"About my mother?" Anthea began.

"So, your mother," Meg said at the same time.

They both stopped, and Anthea gestured for Meg to continue.

"So, your mother," she began again. "You know that my mother keeps track of her, when she can . . . ?"

"I did not know that," Anthea said.

"With her Rose Maidens, right?" Jilly looked eager. "Remember when I tried to tell you they were all spies?" She whispered this loudly to Anthea.

"Only a few of them are spies," Meg said, giving an awkward shrug.

"I wish they all were," Jilly said.

"That's not really necessary," Meg said. She winced. "Or, it really wasn't for most queens. They used to just make sure the queen knew all the important gossip.

"But after your mother . . . well, now they bring my mother whatever information they can find on your mother. Though she is very cagey and they rarely even know where she is. But now."

Meg stopped and noisily sucked in a deep breath. She pulled her green scarf off her hair and shook it out.

"Now," she said. "My mother and her maidens have lost track of her, but they were almost certain about her whereabouts before the Dag struck, and that's what concerns them."

"Oh, no," Anthea said.

Jilly was shaking her head slowly, as though in denial, but when Anthea caught her eye she mouthed a single word. "Tube."

"The Dag struck in Travertine and Bellair almost simultaneously," Meg went on. "Your mother was seen in both towns the same week. And then she was in Harkham, just as it broke out there.

"But the reason why Mother sent you all to Upper Stonesraugh? Your mother went to Camryn, and then disappeared." Meg sighed, looking much older than her years.

"My mother knows that there is a woman who comes and goes from her village. She knows that she gives them information, or finds lost artifacts. But because my mother has tried so hard to hide her true home, she cannot get more than vague reports back from the MagTaran."

Meg looked sad at this, and Anthea thought again with a

pang how hard it must be for the queen to always be hiding her true nature from everyone, including her own husband.

"My mother has long suspected that Genevia Cross was the great benefactress of her old village, so she rather threw caution to the winds. She ordered a Matron in Camryn to follow your mother. Lady Pellegrin lost track of her, but it was within ten miles of Upper Stonesraugh.

"My mother had her letter to Finn ready when she got word that the Dag had reached her village."

Jilly put her arm around Anthea. Anthea would have leaned against her cousin, but frankly she could not move. She was staring over Meg's shoulder, her feet rooted to the ground. Florian tugged his reins free and came to her other side, nuzzling her hair with his soft nose.

"As much as I dislike Anthea's mother," Jilly said. "And absolutely trust and adore and in all ways worship yours," she added to Meg. "I still can't grasp this. How could she?"

"I don't understand it either," Meg whispered. "Does she have the Dag, and she's running around coughing on everyone? Wouldn't she be dead by now?"

"Sadly, that I do understand," Jilly said.

"Blood," Anthea whispered. "Saliva. Sputum."

"I beg your pardon?" Meg's hopeful smile faded and she looked faintly disgusted. "Is sputum what I think it is?"

"It is," Jilly said, "and we've found one of the vials she used to transport it."

"Yes," Anthea said. "All she would need is a quick trip to a hospital. Or to snoop around Dr. Rosemary's college. And then once it really gets going, once she starts to spread it, she would have more samples, fresher samples."

"Please don't ever say 'fresher samples' again," Jilly said shakily. "Unless you are talking about marzipan." She looked at Meg. "Where is the horrible—sorry, Thea—Mrs. Cross-Thornley now?"

"Cross," Anthea said. "Genevia Cross." She stroked Florian's mane a little too savagely, and tugged out some hairs by accident. She kissed his neck to apologize. "She's not a Thornley, not anymore. I refuse to allow it."

"Why is she doing all this?" Jilly appealed to them both. "Why is she killing people? With a disease? I mean . . . Who . . . why?"

"She's ruining any chance we have of horses being accepted in the south," Anthea said dully. "She wants them all killed."

"Oh, Anthea, I'm so sorry," Jilly said. "She's just so . . . and you're so . . ."

"Um, I don't think she wants to kill the horses," Meg said.

Anthea, who had been lying against Florian's neck and breathing hard, looked up at the princess sharply. Her stir of emotions made Florian whinny and stamp his feet, but he was careful not to move away from her and throw her off balance. She clutched at his mane.

"What else do you know?" Anthea whispered.

"I'm not even supposed to know this," Meg said cautiously.

"But Bel—my sister Annabel, that is—she and I . . . well, sometimes we pretend to be Rose Maidens."

"And spy?" Jilly asked eagerly.

"And spy," Meg admitted. "And when those Kronenhofer ships were destroyed, and all the angry letters were going back and forth? We wanted to know if we were going to war or not."

All the horses shifted uneasily.

"We are, probably," Meg admitted. "But the thing we remember most was about the horses. One of the Kronenhofer emperor's letters talked about how he wasn't going to buy our horses anymore. He said he had something better, anyway, and he could take what he wanted from us. My father was worried about that last bit, what does he have that's 'better.' But Bel and I, we couldn't understand why he said he wouldn't buy our horses because—"

"Who offered to sell him our horses?" Jilly said indignantly.

"My mother, that's who," Anthea said angrily.

"So the horses that didn't die from the Dag were supposed to go to Kronenhof," Jilly said slowly. "Giving her a lovely fortune, I'm sure."

"But she didn't know the horses were inoculated," Meg said. "None of them died, right?"

"That's right," Jilly said.

"She's already rich," Anthea said. "Her mother, Uncle Daniel's father . . . she inherited so much! Why is she doing this?"

Meg sucked in a breath and let it out again. "Emily, my oldest sister? She told Annabel, and Bel told me, that . . . well,

Emily hates your mother because she thinks that she wants to marry Father. Or she used to."

"What?" Jilly eyes were round.

"Maybe now she's flirting with the emperor?" Meg made a face.

Anthea couldn't even think about that.

"How is she planning on getting the horses to Kronenhof?" she whispered. "There's got to be more to her plan than this. When was she planning to steal them?"

"I don't know," Meg said. "None of us do. But my mother said it's better for you all to know everything, so that you can be on your guard."

"I love your mother," Jilly said simply.

Anthea wanted to agree, but found she was fighting a lump in her throat.

"What does your father say about all this?" Jilly asked.

She shot Anthea a sympathetic look, and Anthea used her cousin's question as cover to get a grip on herself. She checked the horses' water and gave them all extra pats on the neck, even though Meg's answer gave her pause.

"He doesn't know that we know," Meg admitted. "He won't talk about Mistress Cross-Thor—Mistress Cross. At all. With anyone. And of course we didn't dare tell him we were eavesdropping."

"Spying," Jilly corrected her. "It's sounds more dangerous. And exciting."

"Exactly."

"What if he finds out?" Anthea managed to say. "That your mother knows all this? That she sent letters to us, to Finn? About the village?" She could feel the tension knotting her shoulders.

"She says she will fight that battle when it comes, and not before," Meg said uneasily. "And that she's done putting up with his tantrums." She made a face. "I guess . . . we just have to let her do it."

They all had to think about that silently for a moment. Anthea didn't know if she could shoulder any more worries about the queen, about the future. About her own mother.

"Where were you going?" Anthea asked finally. "If we hadn't caught you?"

"To Upper Stonesraugh," Meg said. "Well, I was told to go to Lady Pellegrin in Camryn and see if Blossom could reach you from there. But I was going to go to the village instead." She gave them a shy smile. "You and Jilly are supposed to come with me."

"Back to Bell Hyde?"

"No."

Meg went to her saddlebag and pulled something out. It was a small velvet bag. She tipped two shining things onto her palm and held them up.

"Like I said, my mother has decided that it's time to stop dancing around my father and his tantrums," Meg said grimly. "She has asked me to give you these."

Anthea and Jilly leaned over to look. There were two

shining gold brooches in Meg's palm. They were U-shaped rosebuds, like the queen's personal seal, but there was a horseshoe around each one, plain as could be. A single diamond was set in the tips of the rosebud's petals, like a drop of dew.

Meg straightened and cleared her throat, her arm still outstretched.

"Her Majesty Queen Josephine has asked me to invite you to travel to the cities of Coronam and read a letter from her, absolving horses of any part in the Dag. She wishes you to further instruct the people in the Way, and look for those who may have it.

"And it is her wish that you accept these brooches as a symbol of your new status, as the Queen's Own Horse Maidens."

20

HORSE MAIDENS AT LARGE

"THEY'RE SHOOTING AT US!" Meg screamed.

They charged down the road, letting the horses have their heads.

"I'm going to shoot back!" Jilly shouted, turning in the saddle.

"Jilly, don't!"

Anthea cried out in a panic as her cousin pulled her pistol out of her embroidered coat. She crouched low on Florian's neck, waiting to feel the burning punch of a bullet entering her side again. Anthea whipped at Leonidas with the end of her reins. They had to get out of there before someone shot them or worse: Jilly killed someone.

The townspeople followed them much farther than Anthea would have thought. At least they were on foot, not in motorcars, and soon they fell behind the three girls on their horses.

Anthea still kept them running as long as she dared, though. Just in case. Just to be sure. But the horses were tired already, and finally she signaled for them to slow to a walk. They had automatically gone north when they left the town, and now they came to another crossroads and Anthea pointed them north and west without asking.

"You should have let me shoot at them," Jilly grumbled.

"How would that have helped?" Anthea asked.

"It would have made *me* feel better!"

"They shot at us," Meg said. "They shot at *me*. I'm a *princess*, and they *shot* at *me*."

"Last year some farmers shot Anthea so that they could keep Florian," Jilly pointed out. "They didn't even know *what* he was."

"I remember when you came to Bell Hyde the first time," Meg said. "I remember . . . I thought . . . did the hunters know you were a girl?"

"Yes, they did," Anthea said shortly.

Anthea let them pore over the details of last year's debacle as they continued to walk up the road. Meanwhile, she thought about what they had just done in the small town of Pickerton.

They had ridden into the center of town, gesturing for those who saw them to come along with them. In the middle of the town, where a large church overlooked a cobbled square, they had stopped and asked to see the mayor. He was already on his way, still weak from the Dag and leaning on the arm of his son.

Most of the town looked as though they had been ill, or were exhausted from caring for the ill, but the sight of three girls on horses clopping down their streets had brought them all to the square.

The people stayed well clear of the horses. Some of them had their children hidden behind them, or were shoving them into the doors of houses and shops and telling them to stay put. Anthea uneasily noticed that there were far more men than women. Had the women died, or were they staying away?

"Good day to you all," Jilly called out cheerily. "My name is Jillian Thornley, and I am one of Her Majesty Queen Josephine's Horse Maidens!"

Gasps rang out. Jilly smiled even more broadly, but Anthea felt cold beneath her heavy coat. Those weren't gasps of awe and amazement. Those were the gasps of respectable people being shocked and offended, a sound she knew all too well.

"Jilly," Anthea whispered.

"I am Princess Margaret," the princess said, urging Blossom forward. "I have here a letter from my mother, the queen—"

"How dare you!"

One of the few women there had shouted out. She had a red patch on one cheek of fresh scars from the Dag. There was a small boy half-hidden in her apron, but now she shoved him into the arms of the man beside her.

"How dare you use the name of our good queen this way?" The woman shook her fist at them. "How dare you use her name to come here and spread this filthy plague! Is it not enough that hundreds of us are dead? Do you have to kill the rest and defame the queen, too?"

That was when several of the men had pulled out guns. That was when the Pickerton constables had moved to the front of the crowd. When Meg had shrilly insisted that she was a princess, and someone had spat at her.

That was when Anthea, her heart in her throat, heard a memory of a gunshot and felt the ghost of a pain in her side. She spun her horse around, and began to ride, straight back the way they had come, straight out of that town.

The others followed her, and the townspeople followed them, and there were warning shots fired over their heads. They didn't get a chance to show off their new brooches, or leave any medicine, or ask what else the people might need. They could only run, and keep running.

"Where to next?" Jilly asked as they stopped at a crossroads. She pulled a map out of her saddlebags and unfolded a portion.

"We're going to Upper Stonesraugh," Anthea said. Her heart was still hammering.

"Along the way we would hit quite a few towns," Jilly said. She pulled a pencil out of her pocket and started to make notes.

"A *few* towns?" Meg sounded panicky. Blossom whickered and ramped sideways a little, sensing her rider's mood. "How many is a few?"

"They won't all be like this," Jilly said breezily.

"They will," Anthea said.

She rubbed Florian's neck. Then she reached over and stroked Leonidas as well. Her heart broke a little. How could people not love these beautiful creatures on sight?

"My mother has done her work too well," Anthea said. She didn't add, "And so has your father," not wanting to hurt Meg's feelings.

Anthea felt a tear slip down her cheek.

Beloved.

I'm all right.

You are not.

I didn't think it would still hurt so much.

"Well," Jilly said. "What should we do? We have to press on!"

"To Upper Stonesraugh," Anthea said, choking on the name because of the thickness in her throat.

Jilly looked at Anthea, her mouth open. "Are you *crying*?"

Anthea steeled herself for the teasing, but instead she looked over to see Jilly reining in Caesar, pulling him close to Florian. Jilly dropped her reins and threw her arms around Anthea.

"It will be okay," Jilly said.

"It won't," Anthea said. "It just won't! We're going to fight this battle all our lives and we'll never win." She began to sob, huge ugly gasps, heaving into her cousin's shoulder.

"Get down," Jilly said. "We'll fall!"

"Florian won't let me," Anthea hiccupped. "I can't fall off Florian."

I would never let you fall, Florian said, stung by Jilly's words.

I am sure she only meant that I would make her *topple off*, Anthea soothed him.

Nevertheless, Anthea got herself together, and managed to sit up straight. She took out a handkerchief and mopped her face. Then she offered another to Jilly, whose coat was honestly so tightly fitted that Anthea wasn't sure it still had pockets.

"Can . . . can we just go straight to my mother's village?" Meg asked, turning Blossom in a tight, nervous circle. She seemed even more upset by Anthea's weeping than she had been by being shot at.

"We really, really should," Anthea said.

"Can't we try even one more?" Jilly wheedled. "Just a tiny village?"

"We can't," Anthea decided.

She had been worrying about something the entire journey away from Upper Stonesraugh. She had been distracted by Meg joining them, distracted by the new Horse Maiden brooch that graced her coat. Distracted by their reception in Pickerton.

But she could not be distracted anymore.

"Finn has not sent a message," she said. "At all. Nothing. No all is well, or I found an amazing book. Nothing. Nor has Caillin MacRennie."

"We are very far away," Meg said doubtfully. "Aren't we?"

"Not too far for Constantine," Anthea said. "They should have sent a message by now. He should have brought Constantine out of the standing stones to let us know they were all right."

"Constantine?" Meg said in shock. "Finn brought Constantine south of the Wall again?"

"Well, your mother told him to," Jilly said. She put her map away and turned Caesar toward the left-hand branch of the road.

"No she didn't," Meg said, turning Blossom to follow Caesar. "She never would have endangered Finn and Constantine."

"I've seen the letter," Jilly said. "She clearly said to ride Constantine there, and show him to the villagers."

"No, in Thea's letter she advised her to take Florian," Meg argued. "So that the people could see how strong their bond was. But in Finn's she said to leave the herd stallion home."

"What letter?" Anthea pulled up. "She hasn't sent me a letter since days before Finn was told about the village."

"She showed me both," Meg said, reining in Blossom and looking back at Anthea in confusion. "She sent them at the same time. She hadn't gotten very many letters from you since the Dag spread so much; she thought you were just busy, but she never would have sent a letter to Finn and not to you, too." Meg wrinkled her nose. "I've honestly been a little jealous of you, and Jilly," she admitted.

Normally Anthea would have been flattered. Normally she

would have rushed to reassure the younger girl. But she was frozen in place.

Beloved?

Someone stole my letters, my love. Someone changed Finn's letter.

"We have to get to the Last Village right now," Jilly said in a strangled voice.

21

THE FIRE BURNING

THEY WERE STILL A day's ride from Upper Stonesraugh when it happened. Jilly was just telling Meg about Caillin Mac-Rennie, and saying that they would soon be at the abandoned tower where they had left him.

"But, has *he* checked in?" Meg asked.

"Yes," Jilly said. "Until we went a little too far south."

"But he hasn't since we got closer," Anthea said grimly. "I have been having Florian hail Brutus since last night, and he has no clue where Brutus is."

"He's probably gone to help Finn," Jilly said.

That made them all fall silent. If Finn needed help, and Caillin MacRennie had gone to him . . . That was just confirmation that something was wrong, wasn't it?

Suddenly the road rippled. Everything rippled, and Anthea

heard a crash and a cry. She clutched tight to Florian's neck. He stopped, all four legs braced.

Leonidas whinnied and half fell, half leaned into Florian, pressing Anthea's leg painfully into the saddle. The other horses all stumbled or stopped dead, including Blossom. Meg slid unceremoniously off her mare and landed in a heap on the road with a small cry.

Anthea freed her leg so that she could dismount and help, even though Jilly was already on the ground and hurrying to tell Meg to get back up and remount. Anthea had one foot out of the stirrup and was swinging it over Florian's rump when it hit her.

Help! She's here! Quickly!

Anthea fell the rest of the way out of the saddle, but her left foot stayed in the stirrup. She landed hard on her back with her feet in the air, accidentally kicking Florian in the side with her flailing right leg.

He leaped forward, startled, and dragged her a little. Leonidas rushed to cut him off before he could drag Anthea very far.

"You fell, too?"

Jilly's face was incredulous as she came around the two stallions and looked at Anthea. Then she freed Anthea's foot from the stirrup and let it fall to the ground with a thud.

"Did you hear that?" Anthea whispered.

"What?" Jilly didn't bother to whisper. "Everyone but me falling?"

"I need a leg up," Meg said, still sounding out of breath.

Thea! Thea?

"Do you hear that?" Anthea demanded.

She lurched to her feet. Her heavy coat and leather gloves had prevented her from being scraped by the dragging, but she had grit and dirt in her already dirty hair, she was sure, and she was bruised and still a little winded.

But this took precedence: she could hear someone speaking to her through the Way. And she didn't think it was a horse.

"Jilly." Anthea grabbed her cousin's arm. "Did. You. Hear. That?"

"I *felt* something, but I didn't *hear* anything," Jilly said. "It felt like an earthquake," she added.

"An earthquake?" Meg squeaked. "I didn't think we had those in Coronam!"

Beloved? It was not an earthquake, Florian said.

The Now King, Leonidas said, looking anxiously up the road. *We must go!*

Finn?

Anthea wasn't sure whom she was talking to, the horses or the boy. She didn't really care.

Finn? Finn!

"I'm going to boost you onto Florian," Jilly announced. "We need to go, whatever is happening."

Caillin MacRennie! Anthea called now.

She absentmindedly took the reins and let Jilly grab her leg and hoist her toward her saddle with much grunting. Florian dipped his shoulder and bent his knees and Anthea found herself more or less in the saddle. Jilly did the same thing for Meg, but Anthea was only vaguely aware of this. As soon as her rear end had hit the saddle, Florian was moving. She put her feet into the stirrups and adjusted her long coat as they walked up the road.

Leonidas's lead line had come loose from Florian's saddle, but he followed with his head at Anthea's knee, his ears straining forward. Anthea reached out and grabbed his bridle, then gathered up the lead so that he wouldn't trip on it. She unfastened it and shoved it into one of his saddlebags. Leonidas actually stopped and then hurried forward again, snorting.

You are a good and loyal stallion, Anthea told him. *I know that you will follow me. And I know that you will run if I tell you to run.*

Run?

To the north, to the farm, she told him. *If the danger is too great, if we need to get a message to the farm, can you go alone?*

I . . . I can.

Good, very good.

"We should do a gallop," Jilly said.

They did. They walked and trotted and galloped as best they could without hurting the horses. When they passed the tower where Caillin MacRennie should have been, Anthea told them to keep going. She could not sense any horses except their own, and that meant that Caillin MacRennie was gone as well.

They stopped to eat, to feed the horses, and then they

kept riding. It snowed a little, then rained, and they kept riding. They were all tired, but they knew they had to keep going, even though they hadn't heard anything from Finn since those first cries.

Then they turned down the road to Upper Stonesraugh.

Florian started to gallop and Anthea did nothing to stop him. It was dark, the road was terrible, and they were exhausted and scared. But now they could all hear it.

Stop her!

What is happening?

Guard the king! Guard the king!

No good!

What is that?

Thea! Thea, run!

The words jumbled around in Anthea's brain. Some were from horses, others from humans, but it was almost impossible to tell which was which. It was obvious that the horses, and the other girls, were hearing these things as well.

Meg looked like she might swoon, and Anthea sent a message to Blossom to fall back if she needed to keep her rider in the saddle. They had been riding so hard and so long that it was almost dawn again, and Anthea knew that they should stop and approach with greater caution, but one glance at Jilly told her that she wasn't the only one anxious to keep moving. Anthea had never seen her cousin's face look so serious, not even when Uncle Andrew had gotten sick with the Dag.

With the dawn coming on behind them, they reached the

rim of standing stones and looked down on the destruction of the valley that held Upper Stonesraugh.

"What happened?" Jilly said in a hushed voice.

Constantine is not here, Florian said.

"The manor is on fire," Anthea choked out. "Finn!"

Come quick! Finn's voice shouted in Anthea's mind. *Past the manor! She's taken Constantine! Your mother has Constantine!*

22

A MONSTROUS MACHINE

THEY ABANDONED THE PACKHORSES, to follow as they could. Anthea had already freed Leonidas, so he just stayed alongside Florian, but Jilly had to stop and untie Buttercup, and Meg and Blossom were moving very slowly.

Or so it seemed to Anthea.

She and Florian were both tired, but they found the strength to race along the track that outlined the village, the same path they had used before, running along behind the cottages and the pig sties and the chicken coops. But this time there was a difference. This time there were people.

There were children hovering in doorways, as though they'd been told to stay inside but wanted to watch. There were women with their sleeves rolled back and their faces flushed despite the cold, with buckets in their hand. There was a pair of elderly men carrying a washtub between them so that they could use their canes.

And every single one of them, when they saw Anthea, pointed toward the manor house. Two little girls in white pinafores daringly leaped out of the door of their cottage and cheered, then darted back inside.

Anthea didn't know what they were cheering about. She could already smell the fire. Looking up through Florian's ears she saw the smoke billowing over the church, and knew exactly where and why the women and the old men were bringing buckets and washtubs.

The manor was on fire.

Dear Anthea, Leonidas said.

I know, my brave one, come when you can.

Never as strong or as fast as Florian, Leonidas faded back. Out of the corner of her eye she could see Caesar's nose as he and Jilly caught up.

Leonidas, guard the mares, Anthea ordered. *Stay with Buttercup and Blossom and keep them together. Guard the New Meg.*

I will.

Then she came around the tall trees of the churchyard, and hauled back on Florian's reins. The manor wasn't on fire. The manor was destroyed.

The front of it was simply gone. A gaping hole had been blasted in the beautiful stone façade, and there were flames pouring out of it. The villagers had formed a bucket line and were trying to put out the fire, shouting for more buckets, more washtubs, more water, as two of the men frantically worked the old well at the edge of the garden and another took his turn at the more modern pump near the side of the manor.

And there, streaked black and far too close to the fire for Anthea's comfort, was Caillin MacRennie. He was shouting orders and tossing water, while the MagTaran stood at his shoulder looking like he'd been stunned by a blow to the head.

Anthea stood in her stirrups.

"Caillin MacRennie!" she screamed.

His head whipped around, but he threw the bucket he'd just emptied to the man next to him without missing a beat.

"Go!" he shouted, and his voice cracked with smoke or emotion. "Go! Follow the trail! Get the boy!"

"Trail?" Anthea shouted back, confused.

"There!" Jilly was pointing to the side.

It wasn't the kind of trail Anthea was expecting. It was a great, torn-up swath of the earth that cut around the side of the manor. The stone wall around the manor garden had been flattened, and the torn-up earth led on and away, toward the far end of the village.

"What did this?" Jilly said.

They had to slow down, not just because the horses could no longer keep running, but because of the treacherous, torn-up ground. Rocks from the wall had been scattered into the muck, and uprooted shrubs as well.

There were tracks in the muck, like the tracks of a motorcar, but not. A continuous trail of strange tire marks, twice as wide as any car, wider than a train, and so heavy that many of the stones had been pushed deep into the hard earth. Anthea thought of the voices she had heard, the ones crying out, *What is it?*

All she could do was shake her head at Jilly. They had to get to Finn. They had to protect the last King of Leana, the Soon King. The Now King.

That nearly brought her up short. They were traveling with a human princess and mares. Two types of creature that were cherished and protected in Coronam *and* Leana.

Leonidas! You must *guard the New Meg and the mares! Don't come with us! Take them to a corner of the manor garden, away from the fire, and wait for Caillin MacRennie to take care of you. Tell Blossom to tell the New Meg that she must stay. It is not safe!*

I will.

She passed her decision to Jilly via Caesar, since they had had to go wide around each side of a torn up tree and she didn't want to shout. Then Anthea sent her mind searching ahead, looking for Constantine, for Marius, for Finn.

She could not find Constantine, but there was a flicker that she was sure was Marius. She told Florian to reach out to him, to see how far away they were, as they started up the rise toward the standing stones.

One of the stones was gone.

At first Anthea thought it had just been knocked down by whatever had smashed its way through the valley. But when they went to pass through the ring, it was just gone. There was no way a stone of that size could have been pushed so deep into the ground that they couldn't have seen some trace of it.

As they passed through the gap left, Anthea realized that there was no ripple. There hadn't been going into the valley either, she remembered. The ring of stones had been broken, and that had stolen whatever power it had had. It was why she had suddenly heard the voices, asking for help, telling her to run.

But whose voices had they been? Marius and Finn she was sure of. Caillin MacRennie? Constantine? One of the voices had been female, she was almost certain, but there were no mares in the village. One of the village women, then? If they really were all Leanan, full-blooded Leanan, could they all have the Way so strongly?

"Anthea, look!" Jilly pointed ahead of them.

At the same time, they heard Finn's voice in their ears and Marius's voice in their heads. They also heard a terrible grinding, crashing sound. And ahead of them they saw Finn, riding Marius flat out, in the wake of a terrible gray metal thing that was ripping apart the forest in front of it.

Florian skidded to a halt, and so did Caesar. Their minds were pure panic, and Anthea didn't blame them. What *was* that thing? It was like a motorcar and a train and some sort of iron-sided navy ship all rolled into one.

Shaped like a huge steel box, there was a long gray tube mounted on the top that Anthea was fairly certain was some sort of cannon. She couldn't see any windows, and had no idea how the machine could see where it was going. Instead of wheels it had big steel treads that rolled over everything in its wake without making a bump.

"Finn, stop!" Anthea screamed. "Come away!"

Marius turned and came back to them, though Finn tugged on the reins and swore. Marius was the one too scared to continue, and Florian and Caesar would not take one step closer to the iron beast. Finn sagged in the saddle when Marius stopped, lathered and blowing, to face Florian.

"She took Constantine," Finn said dully.

His face was so pale beneath the streaks of sweat and soot on his cheeks, his hair so thick with dust and ash that he looked like a photograph and not a real person at all. He yanked on the reins but Marius refused to budge, and he started to dismount.

Afraid that he would try to face down that machine on foot, and be crushed for his efforts, Anthea reached over and grabbed his arm to stop him. He struggled for a moment but then gave up, slumping even lower.

"Who did this? My mother?" she demanded.

"Yes."

"What is that thing?" Jilly wanted to know.

"They called it a schutzer-something," Finn said. "I couldn't quite hear. It all happened so fast." He blinked rapidly, and sort of leaned toward Anthea. She moved Florian around with her heel and put an arm around Finn.

"Schutzer-something?" Jilly's ears would have pricked up if she had been a horse. "Were they Kronenhofer?"

"I think so," Finn said. "Your mother was speaking another language to them, I think it was Kronenhofer. It sounded like it."

"All right," Jilly said. "You and Marius are tired, but we need to—"

"She started a plague *and* a war?" Anthea practically screamed the words.

Marius shied away from her and she almost pulled Finn off his back. She let go of his shoulders so that she could grip her head with both hands. She felt like her skull was about to explode.

"How is this woman a real person?" Anthea ranted. "How is she even real? How is she my mother?"

"I don't think—" Jilly began in a soothing voice.

"She stole the herd stallion," Finn interrupted. "And Brutus! And Campanula! And she tried to take Marius, too!"

"Why? Why didn't she just shoot them?" Jilly's words made all three horses shift uncomfortably.

"That thing could have done it, too," Finn said, and they all took an uneasy look over their shoulders. "One shot destroyed the front of the manor and the entire library."

"I can't do this," Anthea said, and her teeth started to

chatter. "Jilly, you were wrong . . . I can't hear all the horrible things at once."

"We have to go back," Jilly said, pointing toward Upper Stonesraugh. "Rest, help, plan."

"No!" Finn picked up his reins again. "We have to follow them and—"

"And what? Get shot with a cannon?" Jilly shook her head. "Their trail is perfectly clear, but there's no sense in facing that thing with just some pistols and some tired horses!"

Beloved?

"That's it," Anthea said hotly. "I'm making Florian the herd stallion!"

Beloved, I am—

"I am the king!" Finn shouted at her. "We must go after Con now!"

I cannot! Marius wailed.

His knees buckled and he crashed down into the cold, churned mud, throwing Finn off his back. Jilly gasped and Caesar half reared in shock. Rock steady, Florian lifted his head and trumpeted to get their attention.

Beloved! Now King! She Who Is Jilly! Florian cried out in all their minds. *There is fighting at the manor house! Someone is stealing the mares and the New Meg!*

It cannot be! Caesar cried.

I cannot go on, Marius said.

Leave him, Anthea ordered, though it broke her heart. *Finn, get up here.*

Finn scrambled to his feet and Anthea kicked out of a stirrup and held out her arm. He put a foot in and grabbed her elbow to swing up behind her, and they were off before she could get her own foot back in the stirrup or pull her coat out from under him, with Jilly right beside them on Caesar.

Anthea could hear Marius crying behind them, and felt her heart break even further, but she couldn't stop. They had to find out what was happening at the manor.

When they got there, they saw that the fire was nearly out. Which made it easy to see the back door of the enormous van closing on Buttercup's golden tail, and the crumpled forms of the villagers who had tried to stop the thieves.

Howling with rage, Finn leaped from Florian's back as the van sped off. But there was nothing any of them could do.

CONSTANTINE

Constantine was frightened, but he could not let the mares see. He was also filled with rage, and that he did allow all of them to witness. If they questioned—dared to question—the trembling of his legs or the rolling of his eyes, let them think it only rage that these humans had dared to lay hands on him and other members of his herd.

It was easy to squash the fright and let the anger come forward, because the woman would not stop talking. The Woman Who Smelled of Dead Roses. Constantine had heard Florian speak of her; she was the mother of his rider, That Anthea filly. And now this mother had stolen *him*! The herd stallion! She had taken mares: Buttercup and Blossom and Campanula, and had dared to threaten them with injury! There was also a human filly, fragile and weeping into the mane of Blossom, by whom she was greatly loved. And Brutus, that strong and stoic stallion, ridden by the Caillin MacRennie!

Brutus had leaped to defend his herd stallion, to help guard the mare Campanula, and so had been taken as well. Marius would be punished when Constantine returned, for he had run away and not gone to Constantine's aid. Now they were all, save the coward Marius, in this clanking, grinding, stinking metal machine, and the woman would not stop talking.

She told Constantine that he would be taken from the Now King, *his* king, calling the Now King a "beardless boy" and a "weakling," and telling Constantine that he would be given, like a lump of sugar, to a new king. She spoke of a mighty bearded king in a faraway land who would make Constantine great, who would give him battles to win.

Constantine trembled with rage.

The Woman Who Smelled of Dead Roses had the Way, but yet she understood nothing.

23

SAILING AFTER STOLEN GOODS

"DON'T LOOK SO WORRIED, Thea," Jilly said. "After all, this is the moment you've been dressing for all your life!"

Anthea looked at her cousin, ready to yell, and met Jilly's bright eyes and familiar rakish smile. Anthea just shrugged her army coat tighter around her, covering the sailor collar of her old school blouse even more, and gave a halfhearted scowl.

She turned away from her cousin to look back over the docks. The massive steamship they were about to board was still loading anonymous crates and bundles, and the men had told them to wait far up the docks with their "animals" so that they wouldn't disturb the sailors.

Arthur stirred in her pocket, so she pulled him out and set him on Florian's back to watch the unloading. He climbed Florian's mane to sit between his ears, and Florian sighed deeply and did his best not to mind.

"We're going to do this," Jilly said softly, taking her arm. "We are going to win."

"Yes, we are," Queen Josephine said. She was standing behind them, and she put her arms around both girls and gave them a little squeeze.

"Your Majesty," Uncle Andrew said. "I wish I could tell you how—"

"Don't say another word, Andrew," the queen said. "It is probably against the law to make the queen cry."

"Probably?" Jilly asked.

"There are a lot of laws, Jilly. I can't keep track of them all."

"Is there a law about not keeping horses?" Anthea asked.

She turned a little in the queen's embrace so that she could see her face. The queen's bright blue eyes were too bright: she was on the verge of tears, which made Anthea's own gray eyes prickle.

"There is not," the queen said firmly. "But since no one believes you, Andrew, I am more than happy to take matters into my own hands while you are in Kronenhof."

"What are you going to do?" Finn was at last drawn out of his glum torpor.

"There will be parades," the queen said emphatically. "There will be deliveries of medicine and vaccines to the last few suffering from the Dag. There will be special decrees. There will be unveilings of my new personal symbol."

She pointed with her chin at the rose and horseshoe that both Anthea and Jilly still wore. The queen herself sported the symbol in gold embroidery on both lapels of her riding jacket, and she and four attendant Maidens had all ridden to the docks to see them off. Three of them had the Way, they had proudly told Anthea.

"I'm going to rip that gate right out of the Wall, and make sure that everyone knows about Last Farm," the queen went on, her voice heated. "And that they know that there's a herd in Bell Hyde, and Upper Stonesraugh, too! Caillin MacRennie and I are going to keep the riders busy traveling all around Coronam and Leana, blowing kisses and blessing babies!"

"But, King Gareth—" Andrew began, the frown creases in his forehead deepening.

"Gareth can go jump in the sea for all I care," the queen said with a sharpness that made Jilly's and Anthea's eyes meet, wide. "Our daughter has been kidnapped! And since he doesn't want a war, and we aren't allowed to talk about it, we are going to do this *my* way. With diplomacy. With polite smiles, and pretending that I'm just sending some friends on a social visit to the dear, dear empress, to show off the horses and their riders, and fetch my Meg from her spontaneous Kronenhofer holiday!"

She cleared her throat.

"And I've let Gareth know that this is all his fault. Him and his darling lady spy!"

She squeezed Anthea even tighter. "I'm sorry, Thea dear, but your mother . . . your mother!"

"We all keep saying it like that," Jilly offered.

"She's not my mother," Anthea said fiercely. "Not my *real* mother!"

"Attagirl," Jilly cheered.

Anthea let her head rest on the queen's shoulder. Josephine tilted her face and kissed the top of Anthea's head.

"My dear horse maidens," Josephine whispered. "Will you find my Meg and bring her home?"

"You know we will," Jilly said.

"We will bring them all home," Anthea said, raising her voice so that Finn could hear, too. "Meg and Constantine, Brutus, Blossom, Campanula, Buttercup! And we'll stop this war my mother is trying to start, before it even gets off the ground!"

"They have those schutzer-somethings," Finn said bleakly, "and we have a handful of horses and pistols."

Arthur hooted softly.

Finn almost smiled. "And an owl."

"I beg your pardon, but that is no way for a king to talk!" a woman's voice cut in. "I can see that this is going to be a lot more work than I was told!"

Anthea went rigid. For a moment she thought it was her mother and her hand moved to her pistol as Josephine let go of her.

But this woman was not as tall or as slender as her mother; though she did have a very large veiled hat pinned to her beautifully upswept hair. She wore a navy blue suit and her high-buttoned boots had violet heels that matched the violet roses embroidered around the high collar of her snowy white silk blouse. Behind her was an entire army of servants bearing dozens of pieces of matching luggage. One of them, Anthea saw, was bearing a basket with not one but two small dogs peeping out.

"Now!" The woman pointed a gloved finger at Finn. "Shoulders back, chin up! There's no need to smile, but there's also no need to scowl!"

"Who are you?" Finn demanded.

Uncle Andrew suddenly gripped Jilly's arm with one hand, drawing her to his side. He turned to Queen Josephine, his mouth open and his face white with shock.

"I'm so sorry, Andrew," the queen said. "I kept thinking I would warn you, but then I didn't know how! This is the best way to make this look like a social visit, you know it is!"

"And I'm so worried about Meg," she added. "I will do anything to get her back!"

"Margaret," the woman said. "Your daughter's name is Margaret, Your Majesty. Pet names are so very inappropriate!"

"Who are you?" Now it was Anthea's turn to ask.

"I'm a lot of things," the woman said with a laugh. "When the queen was merely another Rose Candidate, and I had been elevated to the position of Maiden, I took her under my wing and taught her the ways of the court. I rather fancy that her current high station in life is my doing."

The woman lowered her eyes with calculated modesty, and Anthea thought wildly that she had surely gone to

Miss Miniver's Rose Academy. It was Miss Miniver's signature move.

"So I have been asked to attend you on this journey, to teach you all diplomacy as well as introducing you to my old friend Empress Elisabet. I will also be your translator," the woman said briskly. "Kronenhofer is one of the four languages I speak."

"That's . . . good?"

Anthea's comment came out as a question because both Jilly and Uncle Andrew were still pale as ghosts, and Finn was staring around between them all as though he'd been struck over the head. Anthea looked at Josephine, but the queen avoided her gaze.

"Anthea, Jillian," the woman continued. "I've brought clothes for you both. I guessed at the sizes from those photographs of you and your animals that odd little man took. My maids can alter them as needed. I had thought you could wear some of your own things, but now I see that's impossible."

"I like my coat," Anthea said feebly.

"And I *love* mine," Jilly said hotly. "*You* are not *touching* it. You are not going to say *one word* to me, either! You don't have the *right* to even *look* at me!"

"Oh," Anthea said. "No."

The woman looked at her with one carefully plucked eyebrow raised. "Did you just catch on?" She tsked. "I thought you were supposed to be the smart one!"

"Cassandra!" Uncle Andrew said sharply.

"That's . . . She's really . . ." Finn stammered.

Jilly rounded on Queen Josephine. Her face had gone from white to red.

"I am not going anywhere with *my mother*!"

ACKNOWLEDGMENTS

Middle books, like middle children, have a lot of work to do! They have to support their older and younger siblings, and still manage to shine a light of their own, which is why I'm happy to dedicate this book to my daughter, who is the only girl *and* the middle child!

Because the first book was so long in the works, making its way from childhood journal to WWI story to fantasy at an elegant trot, book two had to wait its turn for quite a while, and then it was time to gallop! A big thank-you to my lovely agent, Amy Jameson, for her constant steady encouragement, and for always being there with a keen ear and just the right words. And a twenty-one-horse salute (that's a thing, isn't it?) to Mary Kate Castellani for guiding this story from very rough outline to finished tale of Horses and High Adventure.

Thanks to all the great people at Bloomsbury, who make every one of my books the best it can be, and help me every step of the way. You guys are the best, and I adore you all!

And a big thank-you to all my extended family, who continue to buoy me up and cheer me on, and especially to the husband and kids who get to reap the benefits of my frozen dark chocolate chip addiction.